"I can't believe you're passing up a home-cooked meal, Jace Yeager," Lori said. "Maggie's biscuits are the best around, and probably even better with Cassie helping."

"Please, Daddy. I'll go to bed right on time. I won't argue or anything."

Jace looked back at Lori. It was her first night here, and probably a rough one.

Lori smiled. "Now, that's a hard offer to turn down."

"You're no help," he told Lori.

"Sorry, us girls have to stick together."

That was what he was afraid of. He was losing more than just this round. He hated that he didn't mind one bit.

"Okay, but we can't stay long. We have a bedtime schedule."

"I promise I'll go to bed right on time," Cassie said again, and then took off toward the kitchen.

He looked at a smiling Lori. "Okay, I'm a pushover."

"Buck up, Dad. It's only going to get worse before it gets better."

Suddenly their eyes locked and the amused look disappeared. Lori was the first to speak. "Please, I want you to stay for dinner. I think we both agree that eating alone isn't fun."

"Yes, we can agree on that."

He followed Lori into the kitchen, knowing this woman could easily fill those lonely times. He just couldn't let it happen. No more women for a while—at least not over the age of seven.

Dear Reader

I can't tell you how happy I am to be returning to Destiny for my next story. The small Colorado town has always been one of my favourite locations—so, for those of you who remember, I'll also be revisiting the Keenan family and their historical inn.

This time I move on to another famous family in town: the Hutchinsons. A hundred years ago Raymond Hutchinson built the mining town after he struck gold in the area. When great-grandson Lyle passes away suddenly his estranged daughter, Lorelei, returns to town for the first time in twenty years to learn she's the only heir to the family fortune. There's a catch. Lori must live in Destiny for a year and run the Hutchinson Corporation. That brings her face to face with angry contractor Jace Yeager.

Jace doesn't have time to deal with any more delays on his construction project—especially when his new partner could stop the project at any time. His first priority is his seven-year-old daughter and getting permanent custody. He doesn't want or need any other female in his life. So it's strictly business with Lorelei Hutchinson—until they're snowed in together…

Enjoy!

I love to hear from my readers, you can read more f Patricia's books set in Destiny?

Look for the original Rocky Mountain Bride trilogy—
Family.
The Sheriff's Pregnant Wife
Mother for the Tycoon's Child

SINGLE DAD'S HOLIDAY WEDDING

BY
PATRICIA THAYER

First published in Great Britain 2012
by Mills & Boon, an imprint of Harlequin (UK) Limited.
Harlequin (UK) Limited, Eton House, 18-24 Paradise Road,
Richmond, Surrey TW9 1SR

© Patricia Wright 2012

ISBN: 978 0 263 22813 7

Harlequin (UK) policy is to use papers that are natural, renewable
and recyclable products and made from wood grown in sustainable
forests. The logging and manufacturing process conform to the
legal environmental regulations of the country of origin.

Printed and bound in Great Britain
by CPI Antony Rowe, Chippenham, Wiltshire

Originally born and raised in Muncie, Indiana, **Patricia Thayer** is the second of eight children. She attended Ball State University, and soon afterwards headed West. Over the years she's made frequent visits back to the Midwest, trying to keep up with her growing family.

Patricia has called Orange County, California, home for many years. She not only enjoys the warm climate, but also the company and support of other published authors in the local writers' organisation. For the past eighteen years she has had the unwavering support and encouragement of her critique group. It's a sisterhood like no other.

When she's not working on a story, you might find her travelling the United States and Europe, taking in the scenery and doing story research while thoroughly enjoying herself, accompanied by Steve, her husband for over thirty-five years. Together, they have three grown sons and four grandsons. As she calls them: her own true-life heroes. On rare days off from writing you might catch her at Disneyland, spoiling those grandkids rotten! She also volunteers for the Grandparent Autism Network.

Patricia has written for over twenty years, and has authored more than forty-six books. She has been nominated for both a National Readers' Choice Award and the prestigious RITA® Award. Her book NOTHING SHORT OF A MIRACLE won an *RT Book Reviews* Reviewers' Choice award.

A longtime member of Romance Writers of America, she has served as President and held many other board positions for her local chapter in Orange County. She's a firm believer in giving back.

Check her website, www.patriciathayer.com, for upcoming books.

Recent books by Patricia Thayer:

THE COWBOY COMES HOME*
ONCE A COWBOY...**
TALL, DARK, TEXAS RANGER**
THE LONESOME RANCHER**
LITTLE COWGIRL NEEDS A MOM**

*The Larkville Legacy
**The Quilt Shop in Kerry Springs

To my Vine Street Sisters.
I've enjoyed our time together. Bless you all.

CHAPTER ONE

SHE still wasn't sure if coming here was a good idea.

Lorelei Hutchinson drove along First Street to the downtown area of the small community of Destiny, Colorado. She reached the historic square and parked her rental car in an angled spot by a huge three-tiered fountain. The centerpiece of the brick-lined plaza was trimmed with a hedge and benches for visitors. A pathway led to a park where children were playing.

She got out, wrapped her coat sweater tighter against the cold autumn temperature and walked closer to watch the water cascade over the marble structure. After nearly twenty years many of her memories had faded, but some were just as vivid as if they'd happened yesterday.

One Christmas she remembered the fountain water was red, the giant tree decorated with multicolored lights and ornaments and everyone singing carols. She had a family then.

A rush of emotions hit her when she recalled being in this exact spot, holding her father's hand as he took her to the park swings. One of the rare occasions she'd spent time with the man. He'd always been too busy building his empire. Too busy for his wife and daughter. So many times she had wanted just a little of his attention, his love. She never got it.

Now it was too late. Lyle Hutchinson was gone.

With a cleansing breath, she turned toward the rows of storefront buildings. She smiled. Not many towns had this step-back-into-the-nineteen-thirties look, but it seemed that Destiny was thriving.

The wind blew dried leaves as she crossed the two-lane street and strolled past Clark's Hardware Store and Save More Pharmacy, where her mother took her for candy and ice cream cones as a child. A good memory. She sure could use some of those right now.

There was a new addition to the block, a bridal shop called Rocky Mountain Bridal Shop. She kept walking, past an antiques store toward a law office with the name Paige Keenan Larkin, Attorney at Law, stenciled on the glass.

She paused at the door to the office. This was her father's town, not hers. Lyle Hutchinson had made sure of that. That was why she needed someone on her side. She pushed the door open and a bell tinkled as she walked into the reception area.

The light coming through the windows of the storefront office illuminated the high ceilings and hardwood floors that smelled of polish and age, but also gave off a homey feeling.

She heard the sound of high heels against the bare floors as a petite woman came down the long hall. She had dark brown hair worn in a blunt cut that brushed her shoulders. A white tailored blouse tucked into a black shirt gave her a professional look.

A bright smile appeared. "Lorelei Hutchinson? I'm Paige Larkin. Welcome home."

* * *

After exchanging pleasantries, Lori was ushered into a small conference room to find a middle-aged man seated at the head of the table, going through a folder. No doubt, her father's attorney.

He saw her and stood. "Lorelei Hutchinson, I'm Dennis Bradley."

She shook his offered hand. "Mr. Bradley."

When the lawyer phoned her last week, and told her of her father's sudden death and that she'd been mentioned in his will, she was shocked about both. She hadn't seen or talked with her father since she'd been seven years old.

All Lori was hoping for now was that she could come into town today, sign any papers for Lyle's will and leave tomorrow.

The middle-aged attorney began, "First of all, Lorelei, I want to express my condolences for your loss. Lyle wasn't only my business associate, but my friend, too." He glanced at Paige and back at her. "I agreed to see you today knowing your reluctance. Your father wanted the formal reading of his will at Hutchinson House tomorrow."

Great. Not the plans she had. "Mr. Bradley, as you know, I haven't seen my father in years. I'm not sure why you insisted I come here." He'd sent her the airline ticket and reserved a rental car. "If Lyle Hutchinson left me anything, couldn't you have sent it to me?"

The man frowned. "As I explained on the phone, Ms. Hutchinson, you're Lyle's sole heir." He shook his head. "And that's all I'm at liberty to say until tomorrow at the reading of the will. Please just stay until then. Believe me, it will benefit not only you, but this town."

Before she could comprehend or react to the news,

the door opened and another man walked into the room. He looked her over and said, "So the prodigal daughter finally made it to town."

The big man had a rough edge to him, his dark hair a little on the shaggy side. He was dressed in charcoal trousers and a collared shirt, minus the tie. His hooded blue-eyed gaze fringed by spiky black lashes didn't waver from her.

Paige stood. "Jace, you shouldn't be here. This is a private meeting between me and my client."

He didn't retreat. "I just wanted to make sure she doesn't take the money and run. Lyle had obligations he needed to fulfill before that happens."

Lori wasn't sure how to handle this—Jace's attack. But having heard of her father's shrewd business deals, she wasn't surprised by the man's anger.

"I'm Lorelei Hutchinson, Mr...."

He stepped closer. "Yeager. Jace Yeager. Your father and I were partners on a construction project until I realized Lyle pulled one over on me."

"Jace," Bradley warned. "Work stopped because of Lyle's death."

The man made a snorting sound. "It wouldn't have if Lyle had put his share of money into the business account in the first place." He glared at Lori. "Sorry if my impatience bothers you, but I've been waiting nearly three weeks and so have my men."

"Be patient a little while longer," Bradley told him. "Everything should be resolved tomorrow."

That didn't appease Mr. Yeager. "You don't understand. I can't keep the project site shut down indefinitely, or I go broke." He turned that heated look on her and she oddly felt a stirring. "It seems tomorrow you're coming into all the money. I want you to know that a chunk of that belongs to me."

Lori fought a gasp. "Look, Mr. Yeager, I don't know anything about your partnership with Lyle, but I'll have Paige look into it."

Jace Yeager had to work hard to keep himself under control. Okay, so he wasn't doing a very good job. When he'd heard that Lorelei Hutchinson was coming today, he only saw red. Was she going to stroll in here, grab her daddy's money and take off? He wasn't going to be on the losing end with a woman again.

Not when his business was on the chopping block, along with his and Cassie's future. Just about every dime he had was wrapped up in this project. And it was already coming to the end of October as it was, with only bad weather on the horizon. It needed to be completed without any more delays.

Jace looked over Lyle's daughter. The pretty blonde with big brown eyes stared back at him. She had a clean-scrubbed look with a dusting of freckles across her nose, and very little makeup.

Okay, she wasn't what he expected, but he'd been wrong about women before. And the last thing he wanted to do was work for her. After his ex-wife, he wasn't going to let another woman have all the control.

He looked at Bradley. "What does Lyle's will say?"

"It won't be read until tomorrow."

Lori saw Jace Yeager's frustration, and felt obligated to say, "Maybe then we'll have some news about the project."

He glared. "There's no doubt I will. I might not have your father's money, Ms. Hutchinson, but I'll fight to keep what's mine."

Jace Yeager turned and stormed out right past a tall redheaded woman who was rushing in. "Oh, dear," she said, "I was hoping I could get here in time." Her green eyes lit up when she saw Lori. "Hi, I'm Morgan Keenan Hilliard."

"Lori Hutchinson," Lori said as she went to shake Morgan's hand.

"It's nice to meet you. As mayor, I wanted to be here to welcome you back to town, and to try and slow down Jace. Not an easy job."

Since Paige and Bradley had their heads together going over papers, they walked out into the hall. "I'm not sure if you remember me."

"I remember a lot about Destiny. Like you and your sisters. You were a little older than I was in school, but everyone knew about the Keenan girls."

Morgan smiled. "And of course being Lyle's daughter, everyone knew of you, too. I hope you have good memories of our town."

Except for her parents' marriage falling apart, along with her childhood. "Mostly, especially the decorated Christmas tree in the square. Do you still do that?"

Morgan smiled. "Oh, yes and it's grown bigger and better every year." She paused. "Our mom said you have a reservation at the inn for tonight."

She nodded. "I don't feel right about staying at the house."

The redhead gripped her hand. "You don't have to explain. I only want your visit here to be as pleasant as possible. If there is anything else, any details about your father's funeral."

Lori quickly shook her head. "Not now."

Morgan quickly changed the subject. "Look, I know

Jace isn't giving you a very good impression at the moment, but he's having some trouble with the Mountain Heritage complex."

"I take it my father was involved in it, too."

Morgan waved her hand. "We can save that discussion for another time. You need to rest after your trip. Be warned, Mom will ask you to dinner…with the family."

Lori wasn't really up to it. She wanted a room and a bed, and to make a quick call back home to her sister.

Morgan must have sensed it. "It's only the family and no business, or probing questions. We'll probably bore you to death talking about kids."

Lori relaxed. She truly didn't want to think about what would happen tomorrow.

"You're right. That's what I need tonight."

That evening as Jace was driving to the Keenan Inn, he came to the conclusion that he'd blown his chance earlier today. He tapped his fist against the steering wheel, angry about the entire mess.

"Daaad, you're not listening."

Jace looked in the rearview mirror to the backseat. "What, sweetie?"

"Do I look all right?"

He glanced over his shoulder. His daughter, Cassandra Marie Yeager, was a pretty girl. She had on stretchy jean pants that covered coltish long legs and a pink sweater that had ruffles around the hem. Her long blond hair had curled around her face with a few tiny braids. Something she'd talked him into helping with.

"You look nice. But you always do."

"We're going to Ellie's grandmother's house. Ellie Larkin is my best friend."

"I think she'll like your outfit."

"What about my hair?"

"Honey, I've always loved your blond curls. The braids are a nice touch."

That brought a big smile to her face and a tightening in his throat. All he ever wanted was for her to be happy.

When they'd moved here six months ago, it hadn't been easy for her. He still only had temporary custody of his daughter. It was supposed to be only during the time when her mother remarried a guy from England. Jace had different plans. He wanted to make Cassie's life here with him permanent. Optimistic that could happen, he went out and bought a run-down house with horse property. Although it needed a lot of work, it felt like the perfect home for them. A couple horses helped coax his seven-year-old daughter into adjusting a little faster to their new life.

A life away from a mother who'd planned to take his Cassie off to Europe. He was so afraid that his little girl would end up in boarding school and he'd only get to see her on holidays.

No, he wouldn't let that happen. A product of the foster care system himself, he'd always longed for a home and family. It hadn't worked out with ex-wife Shelly, and that mistake cost him dearly—a big divorce settlement that had nearly wiped him out. Jace hadn't cared about the money, not if he got his daughter. He only hoped they weren't going to be homeless anytime soon.

His thoughts turned to Lorelei Hutchinson. He didn't like how he reacted to her. Why had she angered him so much? He knew why. She had nothing to do with Lyle's business dealings. But she was due to inherit a lot of money tomorrow, and he could be handed the shaft at the same time. It could cost him everything that mattered. His daughter. No, he wouldn't let that happen.

He pulled up in front of the beautiful three-story Victorian home painted dove-gray with white shutters and trim. The Keenan Inn was a historical landmark, a bed-and-breakfast that was also the home of Tim and Claire Keenan. Jace had heard the story about how three tiny girls had been left with them to raise as their own. That would be Morgan, Paige and Leah. After college all three returned to Destiny to marry and raise their own families.

Right now there was someone else staying in the inn—Lorelei Hutchinson. Somehow he had to convince her that this downtown project needed to move forward. Not only for him, but also for Destiny.

Just then Tim Keenan came out the front door, followed closely by some of their grandkids, Corey, Ellie and Kate.

His daughter grabbed her overnight bag and was out of the car before he could say anything. He climbed out, too.

Tim Keenan waved from the porch. "Hello, Jace."

"Hi, Tim." He walked toward him. "Thank you for inviting Cassie to the sleepover. I think she's getting tired of her father's bad company."

"You have a lot on your mind."

Tim was in his early sixties, but he looked a lot younger. His wife was also attractive, and one of the best cooks in town. He knew that because the Keenans had been the first to stop by when he and Cassie moved into their house. They'd brought enough food for a week.

"Hey, why don't you stay for supper, too?"

He wasn't surprised by the invitation. "Probably not a good idea. I don't think I made much of an impression on Ms. Hutchinson."

The big Irishman grinned. "Have faith, son, and use a little charm. Give Paige a chance to help resolve this." They started toward the door, as Tim continued, "I'm concerned about Lorelei. She wasn't very old, maybe seven, when her parents divorced. Lyle wrote them off, both his ex-wife and his daughter. As far as I know, he never visited her. Now, she has to deal with her estranged father's mess."

Jace felt his chest tighten because this woman's scenario hit too close to home. "That's the trouble with divorce, it's the kids who lose."

They stepped through a wide front door with an etched glass oval that read Keenan Inn and into the lobby. The walls were an ecru color that highlighted the heavy oak wainscoting. A staircase with a hand-carved banister was open all the way to the second floor. All the wood, including the hardwood floors, were polished to a high gloss. He suspected he wasn't the only one who was an expert at restoration.

"This house still amazes me," he said.

"Thanks," Tim acknowledged. "It's been a lot of work over the years, but so worth it. The bed-and-breakfast has allowed me to spend more time with Claire and my girls."

Jace shook his head. "I can't imagine having three daughters."

Keenan's smile brightened. "You have one who gives you joy. I'm a lucky man, I tripled that joy." Tim sobered. "Too bad Lyle didn't feel the same about his child. Maybe we wouldn't be having this conversation tonight."

The sound of laughter drifted in from the back of the house. "That sounds encouraging," Tim said. "Come on, son. Let's go enjoy the evening."

They walked through a large dining room with several small tables covered in white tablecloths for the inn's guests. They continued through a pantry and into a huge kitchen.

Okay, Jace was impressed. There was a large working area with an eight-burner cooktop and industrial-sized oven and refrigerator, and all stainless steel counters, including the prep station. On one side a bank of windows showed the vast lawn and wooded area out back and, of course, a view of the San Juan Mountains. A group of women were gathered at the large round table. He recognized all of them. Morgan because she was married to his good friend Justin Hilliard, another business owner in town. Paige he'd met briefly before today. The petite blonde was Leah Keenan Rawlins. She lived outside of town with her rancher husband, Holt.

And Lorelei.

Tonight, she seemed different, more approachable. She was dressed in nice-fitting jeans, a light blue sweater and a pair of sneakers on her feet. Her hair was pulled back into a ponytail and it brushed her shoulders when she turned her head. She looked about eighteen, which meant whatever he was feeling about her was totally inappropriate.

Those rich, chocolate-brown eyes turned toward him and her smile faded. "Mr. Yeager?"

He went to the group. "It's Jace."

"And I go by Lori," she told him.

He didn't want to like her. He couldn't afford to, not with his future in the balance. "Okay."

"Oh, Jace." Claire Keenan came up to them. "Good, you're able to stay for dinner. We don't get to see enough of you." She smiled. "I get to see your daughter when I volunteer at school."

He nodded. "And I'm happy Ellie and Cassie are friends. Thank you for including her in the kids' sleepovers." He glanced out the window to see his daughter running around with the other children. Happy. "Your granddaughter Ellie helped Cassie adjust to the move here."

Claire's smile was warm. "We all want to make sure you both got settled in and are happy."

That all depended on so many things, he thought. "You've certainly done that."

The older woman turned to Lori. "I wish I could talk you into staying longer. One day isn't much time." Claire looked back at Jace. "Lori is a second grade teacher in Colorado Springs."

Lori didn't want to correct Claire Keenan. She *had* been a second grade teacher before she'd been laid off last month. So she didn't mind that her dear father had decided to leave her a little something. It would be greatly appreciated.

But, no, she couldn't stay. Only long enough to finish up Lyle's unfinished business. She hoped that would be concluded by tomorrow.

Claire excused herself. Tim arrived, handed them both glasses of wine and wandered off, too, leaving them alone.

Lori took a sip of wine, trying not to be too obvious

as she glanced at the large-built man with the broad shoulders and narrow waist. No flab there. He definitely did physical work for a living.

"How long have you lived in Destiny, Mr.... Jace?"

"About six months, and I'm hoping to make it permanent."

She didn't look away. "I'm sure things will be straightened out tomorrow."

"I'm glad someone is optimistic."

She sighed. "Look, can't we put this away for the evening? I've had a long day."

He studied her with those deep blue eyes. "If you'd rather I leave, I will. I was only planning to drop my daughter off."

In the past few hours Lori had learned more about Jace Yeager. She knew that Lyle probably had the upper hand with the partnership. "As long as you don't try to pin me down on something I know nothing about. It isn't going to get us anywhere except frustrated."

He raised his glass in salute. "And I'm way beyond that."

CHAPTER TWO

Two hours later, after a delicious pot roast dinner, Lori stood on the back deck at the Keenan Inn. She'd said her goodbyes to everyone at the front door, but wasn't ready to go upstairs to bed yet.

She looked up at the full moon over the mountain peak and wondered what she was doing here. Couldn't she have had a lawyer back in Colorado Springs handle this? First of all, she didn't have the extra money to spend on an attorney when she didn't have a job and very little savings. She needed every penny.

So this was the last place she needed to be, especially with someone like Jace Yeager. She didn't want to deal with him. She only planned to come here, sign any papers to her father's estate and leave.

Now there was another complication, the Mountain Heritage complex. She had to make sure the project moved forward before she left town. She didn't need to be told again that the project would mean employment for several dozen people in Destiny.

"Why, Dad? Why are you doing this?" He hadn't wanted her all those years, now suddenly his daughter needed to return to his town. How many years had she ached for him to come and visit her, or to send for her.

Even a phone call would have been nice. The scars he'd caused made it hard for his daughter to trust. Anyone.

She felt a warm tear on her cold cheek and brushed it away. No. She refused to cry over a man who couldn't give her his time.

"Are you sad?"

Hearing the child's voice, Lori turned around to find Jace Yeager's daughter, Cassie.

Lori put on a smile. "A little. It's been a long time since I've been here. A lot of memories."

The young girl stood under the porch light. "I cried, too, when my daddy made me come here."

"It's hard to move to a new place."

"At first I didn't like it 'cause our house was ugly. When it rained, the ceiling had holes in it." She giggled. "Daddy had to put pans out to catch all the water. My bedroom needed the walls fixed, too. So I had to sleep downstairs by the fireplace while some men put on a new roof."

"So your dad fixed everything?"

She nodded. "He painted my room pink and made me a princess bed like he promised. And I have a horse named Dixie, and Ellie is my best friend."

Her opinion of Jace Yeager just went up several notches. "Sounds like you're a very lucky girl."

The smile disappeared. "But my mommy might come and make me go away."

Jace Yeager didn't have custody of his daughter? "Does your mom live close?"

The child shook her head. "No, she's gonna live in England, but I don't want to live there. I miss her, but I like it here with Daddy, too."

It sounded familiar. "I'm sure they'll work it out."

The girl studied her with the same piercing blue eyes as her father. "Are you going to live here and teach second grade? My school already has Mrs. Miller."

"And I bet you like her, too. No, I'm not going to teach in town, I'm only here for a visit. My dad died not too long ago, and I have to take care of some things."

"Is that why you were crying, because you're sad?"

"Cassie…"

They both turned around and saw Jace.

"Oh, Daddy," Cassie said.

Jace Yeager didn't look happy as he came up the steps. "Ellie's been looking for you." He studied Lori. "The rest of the girls took the party upstairs."

"Oh, I gotta go." She reached up as her father leaned over and kissed her. "'Bye, Daddy, 'bye, Miss Lori." The child took off.

Jace looked at Lori Hutchinson as his gaze locked on her dark eyes.

Finally Lori broke the connection. "I thought you'd left."

"I'd planned to, but I got caught up at the front porch with the Keenans."

He had wanted to speak to Paige, hoping she could give him some encouragement. She'd said she'd work to find a solution to help everyone. Then she rounded up her husband, Sheriff Reed Larkin, leaving her daughters Ellie and Rachel for Grandma Claire's sleepover.

The other sisters, Morgan and Leah, kissed their parents and thanked them for keeping the kids. He caught the look exchanged between the couples, knowing they had a rare night alone. The shared intimacy had him envious, and he turned away. He, too, planned to leave when he spotted his daughter on the back deck with Lori.

"And I was finishing my coffee." He'd had two glasses of wine at dinner. He had to be extra careful, not wanting to give his ex-wife any ammunition. "Well, I should head home."

She nodded. "Your daughter is adorable."

"Thank you. I think so." Jace had to cool it with Lori Hutchinson. "I just wanted to say something before tomorrow...."

She raised a hand. "I told you, I'll do everything I can to get your project operational again."

He just looked at her.

"Whether you believe it or not, I don't plan to cause any more delays than necessary."

"I wish I could believe that."

"After the meeting, how about I come by the building site and tell you what happened?"

He shook his head. "The site's been shut down. Until this matter is settled, I can't afford to pay the subcontractors. So you see there's a lot at stake for me."

"And I understand that. But I still have no idea what's going to happen tomorrow, or what Lyle Hutchinson's plans are. It's not a secret that I haven't seen the man in years." She blinked several times, fighting tears. "He's dead now." Her voice was hoarse. "And I feel nothing."

Jace was learning quickly that Lyle Hutchinson was a piece of work. "Okay, we can both agree your father was a bastard."

She turned toward the railing. "The worst thing is, you probably knew the man better than I did." She glanced over her shoulder. "So you tell me, Jace Yeager, what is my father planning for me? For his town."

* * *

Tim Keenan stood at the big picture window at the inn as he waved at the last of dinner guests left.

He was a lucky man. He loved his wife and his family. He'd been blessed with a great life running the inn for the past thirty-plus years. Mostly he enjoyed people and prided himself on being able to read body language.

For example, Jace and Lori had been dancing around each other all night. Not too close, but never out of eye sight. And the looks shared between them…oh, my.

Claire came down the steps and toward him, slipping into his arms. "I got the girls settled down for now, but I have a feeling they're plotting against me."

He kissed her cheek. "Not those little angels."

She smiled. "Seems you thought the same about your daughters, too."

"They are angels." He thought about the years raising his girls. And the grandchildren. "And we're truly blessed." He glanced out to see the lonely-looking woman on the porch. Not everyone was as lucky.

Lori watched from the inn's porch as Jace walked to his truck. He was strong and a little cocky. She had to like that about him. She also liked the way he interacted with his daughter. Clearly they loved each other. What about his ex-wife? She seemed to have moved on, in Europe. Who broke it off? She couldn't help but wonder what woman in her right mind would leave a man like Jace Yeager. She straightened. There could be a lot of reasons. Reasons she didn't need to think about. Even though she'd seen his intensity over the project, she'd also seen the gentleness in those work-roughened hands when he touched his daughter.

She shivered. One thing was, he wasn't going to be

put off about the project. And she couldn't wait for this mess to be settled. Then she could put her past behind her and move on.

She walked inside and up to the second floor. Overhead she heard the muffled voices of the kids. Her room was at the front of the house. A large canopy bed had an overstuffed print comforter opposite a brick fireplace. She took out her cell phone and checked her messages. Two missed calls.

Fear hit her as she listened to the message from Gina. She could hear the panic in her half sister's voice, but it had been like that since childhood.

Lori's mother had remarried shortly after moving to Colorado Springs. Not her best idea, losing Lyle's alimony, but Jocelyn was the type of woman who needed a man. She just hadn't been good at picking the right ones. Her short union with Dave Williams had produced a daughter, Regina. Lori had been the one who raised her, until big sister had gone off to college.

Without Lori around, and given the neglect of their mother, Gina had run wild and ended up pregnant and married to her boyfriend, Eric Lowell, at barely eighteen. Except for Gina's son, Zack, her life had been a mess ever since. It became worse when her husband became abusive, though the marriage ended with the man going to jail. Now Lori was tangled up in this mess, too.

She punched in the number. "Gina, what happened?"

"Oh, Lori, I think Eric found us."

Over a year ago, Lori had moved her sister into her apartment while Eric served a jail sentence for drug possession and spousal abuse. This hadn't been the first time he'd smacked Gina around, but the first conviction. That was the reason they'd planned to move out of state when Lori had been notified about Lyle's death.

"No, Gina, he doesn't get out until the first of the month."

"Maybe he got an early release."

"Detective Rogers would have called you. You still have a few weeks."

"What about you? Are you flying home soon?"

She knew this delay would worry Gina more. "I can't yet. I still need to meet with the lawyer tomorrow."

She heard a sigh. "I'm sorry, Lori. You've done so much for us. You have a life of your own."

"No, Gina. You're my sister. Zack is my nephew. I told you, I won't let Eric hurt you again. But I still need a day or so to get things straightened out. Then hopefully we'll have some money to start over and get away from Eric." She prayed that her father had left her something. Since their mother had died a few years ago, there wasn't anything holding them in Colorado Springs. They could go anywhere. "Think about where you and Zack want to move to." Preferably somewhere they needed a second grade teacher.

"No, you decide, Lori. We'll go anywhere you want. We just can't stay here. I won't survive it."

Lori could hear the fear in her voice. "I promise I'll do whatever it takes to keep you safe. Now go get some sleep and give my special guy a kiss from me."

Lori hung up the phone and hoped everything she said was true. Unlike Lyle Hutchinson, she didn't walk away from family.

The next morning, Lori was up early. She was used to being at school ahead of her students to plan the day.

Not anymore. Not since she'd gotten her pink slip at the start of the school year. She'd been told it was because of cutbacks and low enrollment, but she wondered if it was due to the trouble Eric had caused her at the upscale private school where she taught.

No, she couldn't think about that now. She needed to have a clear head for the meeting. Was Lyle Hutchinson as wealthy as people said? Normally she wouldn't care, but it could help both her and Gina relocate to another part of the country. Somewhere Gina could raise Zack without the fear of her ex-husband coming after her again. Enough money so Lori had time to find a job.

She drove her car to the end of First Street. A six-foot, wrought-iron fence circled the property that had belonged to the Hutchinsons for over the past hundred years. Her heart raced as she raised her eyes and saw the majestic, three-story white house perched on the hilltop surrounded by trees. Memories bombarded her as she eased past the stone pillars at the gate entrance. The gold plaque read Hutchinson House.

She drove along the hedge-lined circular drive toward the house. She looked over the vast manicured lawn and remembered running through the thick grass, and a swing hanging from a tree out back. She parked in front of the house behind a familiar truck of Jace Yeager. Oh, no. Was the man following her?

Then she saw him standing on the porch leaning against the ornate wrought-iron railing. He was dressed in jeans and a denim shirt and heavy work boots. Without any effort, this man managed to conjure up all sorts of fantasies that had nothing to do with business.

She pulled herself out of her daydream. What was he doing here?

He came down the steps to meet her.

She got out of her car. "Jace, is there a problem?"

He raised a hand in defense. "Mr. Bradley called me this morning. Said he needed me here for after the reading."

Lori was confused. "Why?"

"I hope it's to tell me it's a go-ahead on the Mountain Heritage project."

They started up the steps when she saw a man in a khaki work uniform come around the side porch. He looked to be in his late sixties, maybe seventies. When he got closer she saw something familiar.

"Uncle Charlie?"

The man's weathered face brightened as he smiled. "You remember me, Miss Lorelei?"

"Of course I do. You built me my tree swing." She felt tears sting her eyes. "You let me help plant flowers, too."

He nodded and gripped her hands in his. "That was a lot of years ago, missy. You were a tiny bit of a thing." His tired eyes locked on hers. "You've turned into a beautiful young lady." His grip tightened. "I'm so sorry about your father."

Before Lori could say anything more, another car pulled up. Paige Larkin stepped out of her SUV. Briefcase in hand, she walked up the steps toward them.

They shook hands and Paige spoke briefly to Charlie before the man walked off. Paige turned to Jace. "So you've been summoned, too."

"I got a call from Bradley first thing this morning."

Paige frowned. "Dennis must have a reason for wanting you here." She turned back to her client. "Let's not speculate until we hear what's in Lyle's will."

Lori nodded and together they walked up to the large porch, where greenery filled the pots on either side of the wide door with the leaded glass panels.

She knew that her great-great-grandfather had built this house during the height of the mining era. It was said that Raymond Hutchinson never trusted banks. That was why he didn't lose much during the Great Depression.

They went inside the huge entry with high-gloss hardwood floors. A crystal chandelier hung from the high ceiling and underneath was a round table adorned with a large vase of fresh-cut flowers. The winding staircase circled up to the second story, the banister of hand-carved oak. Cream and deep maroon brocade wallpaper added a formality to the space.

Lori released a breath. "Oh, my."

She was reminded of Jace's presence when he let out a low whistle. "Nice."

"Do you remember this house?" Paige asked.

"Not much. I spent most of my time in the sunroom off the kitchen."

Paige shook her head. "Well, I wouldn't be surprised if this becomes yours. And then you can go anywhere in it you want."

Lori started to tell her she didn't want any part of this house when a thin woman came rushing into the room. Her gray hair was pulled back into a bun. She looked familiar as she smiled and her hazel eyes sparkled. Lori suddenly recognized her.

"Maggie?" she managed to say.

The woman nodded with watery eyes. "Miss Lorelei."

"I can't believe it." Lori didn't hesitate, and went

and hugged the woman. It felt good to be wrapped in the housekeeper's arms again. Years ago, Maggie had been her nanny.

"It's good to have you home." The older woman stepped back and her gaze searched Lori's face. "How pretty you are."

Lori felt herself blush. She wasn't used to all this attention. "Thank you, Maggie."

The housekeeper turned sad. "I'm so sorry about your father." Then squeezed her hands tighter. "I want you to know he went in his sleep. They said a heart attack. Maybe if we would have been there…"

Lori could only nod. "No. He couldn't be helped." She had no idea this would be so hard.

Dennis Bradley walked down the hall. "Good. You made it." He turned and nodded toward Jace. "Mr. Yeager, would you mind waiting a few minutes until I've gone over the will with Ms. Hutchinson?"

"Not a problem." He looked at Maggie and smiled. "I wonder if you could find a cup of coffee for me."

"I'll bring some out."

Once she left, the lawyer said, "We should get started."

He motioned them down the hall and into an office. Lori paused at the doorway. The walls were a deep green with dark stained wainscoting. The plush carpet was slate-gray. Bradley sat down behind the huge desk that already had a folder open.

After they were seated, the lawyer began, "I'll read through Lyle's requests. His first was that the will be read here at the family home." He handed Paige and her copies. "We can go over any details later."

The lawyer slipped on his glasses. "I don't know if

you knew that Lyle had remarried for a short time about ten years ago."

Nothing about her father surprised her. She shook her head.

"There was a prenuptial agreement, then two years later a divorce." He glanced down at the paper. "Lyle did have one other relative, a distant cousin who lives back in Ohio." He read off the generous sum left to Adam Johnson. Also he read the amount given to the household staff, which included Maggie and Charlie.

"I'm glad my father remembered them," Lori said.

Bradley smiled. "They were loyal to him for a lot of years." He sighed. "Now, let's move on to the main part of the will.

"Lyle Hutchinson has bequeathed to his only living child, Lorelei Marie Hutchinson, all his holdings in Hutchinson Corp." He read off the businesses, including Destiny Community Bank, two silver mines, Sunny Hill and Lucky Day. There were six buildings on First Street, and this house at 100 North Street along with all its contents, the furnishings and artwork.

Lori was stunned. "Are you sure this is right?" She looked down at Paige's copy to see the monetary amount stated. "My father was worth this much?"

Bradley nodded. "Lyle was a shrewd businessman. Maybe it was because your grandfather Billy lost nearly everything with his bad investments and eccentric living. Lyle spent years rebuilding the family name and recouping the money. And he also invested a lot into this town."

Bradley looked at her, then at Paige. "Are there any questions?"

Lori gave a sideways glance to her lawyer.

"I probably will once we go over everything."

Bradley nodded. "Call me whenever you need to. Now, for the rest I think Mr. Yeager should hear this. Do you have any objections, Lorelei?" With her agreement, he went to the door and had Jace come in.

He sat down in the chair next to Lori.

Bradley looked at Jace. "Whatever you thought, Mr. Yeager, Lyle went into the Heritage project honestly. The business complex was to promote more jobs and revenue for the town. He wasn't trying to swindle you. As we all know, his death was sudden and unexpected."

Jace nodded. "Of course I understand, but you have to see my side, too. I need to finish this job, get tenants in and paying rent."

Bradley nodded and looked at Lori. "And that will happen if Lorelei will agree to the terms."

"Of course I'll agree to finish this project."

"There is a stipulation in the will." Bradley paused. "You are the last living heir in the Hutchinson line, Lorelei. And this town was founded by your great-great-grandfather, Raymond William Hutchinson, after he struck it rich mining gold and silver. But other business has been coming to Destiny and your father invested wisely. He wants you to continue the tradition."

"And I will," she promised. "I plan to release money right away so the work on Mountain Heritage complex can resume."

Bradley exchanged a look with Paige, then continued on to say, "Everything your father left you is only yours if you take over as CEO of Hutchinson Corporation… and stay in Destiny for the next year."

CHAPTER THREE

LORI had trouble catching her breath. Why? Why would her father want her to stay here to run his company?

"Are you all right?" Jace asked.

She nodded, but it was a lie. "Excuse me." She got up and hurried from the room. Instead of going out the front door, she headed in the other direction.

She ended up in the large kitchen with rows of white cabinets and marble countertops. Of course it was different than she remembered. The old stove was gone, replaced with a huge stainless steel one with black grates.

Suddenly the smell of coffee assaulted her nose and she nearly gagged.

"Miss Lorelei, are you all right?"

She turned around to see a concerned Maggie. She managed a nod. "I just need some air." She fought to walk slowly to the back door and stepped out onto the porch. She drew in a long breath of the brisk air and released it, trying to slow her rapidly beating heart.

Two weeks ago, she couldn't say she even remembered her life here, or the father who hadn't had any time for her. Then the call came about Lyle's death, and she'd been swept up into a whirlwind of emotions and confusion. She couldn't even get herself to visit his grave site.

"Are you sure you're okay?"

She turned around and found Jace standing in the doorway. A shiver ran through her and she pulled her sweater coat tighter around her. "You were there. Would you be okay?"

He came to the railing. "Hell, with that kind of money, I could solve a lot of problems."

She caught a hint of his familiar scent, soap and just his own clean manly smell. She shifted away. She didn't need him distracting her, or his opinion.

"Easy for you to say, your life is here, and you wouldn't have to pull up and move." Lori stole a glance at him. "Or have Lyle Hutchinson running that life."

Jace didn't know the exact amount of money Lyle had left his daughter, but knew it had to be sizable from the investigation Jace had done before he'd entered into the Mountain Heritage project. And he needed that project to move ahead, no matter what he had to do. "It's only a year out of your life."

She glared at him. "That I have no control of."

He studied her face. She was pretty with her small straight nose and big brown eyes. His attention went to her mouth and her perfectly formed lips. He glanced away from the distraction.

Yet, how could he not worry about Lorelei Hutchinson when her decision could put his own livelihood in jeopardy? His other concern was having any more delays, especially when the weather could be a problem. This was business. Only.

"Look, I get it that you and your father had problems,

but you can't change that now. He put you in charge of his company. Surely you can't walk away."

She sent him another piercing look. "My father didn't have a problem walking away from his daughter."

He tried to tell himself she wasn't his problem. Then he remembered if she didn't take over the company, then that was exactly what he'd have to do. Walk away from Cassie. "Then don't walk away like he did. This town needs Hutchinson Corporation to exist."

"Don't you think I know that?"

He sat on the porch railing facing her. "I know it's a three-hundred-mile move from Colorado Springs, but you'll have a great income and a place to live." He nodded toward the house. Then he remembered. "I know you'll have to give up your teaching job."

She glanced out at the lawn. "That I don't have to worry about. I was laid off when the school year started. I have my résumé out in several places."

Jace felt bad for her, but at the same time was hopeful. "It's a bad time for teachers. So maybe it's time for a change. Why can't you take over your father's company?"

"There's so many reasons I can't even count them. First of all, I'm not qualified. I have limited business experience. I could lose everything by managing things badly."

He felt a twinge of hope. "You can learn. Besides, Lyle has lawyers and accountants for a lot of it. I'll be the person at the construction site. You can check out my credentials. I'm damn good at what I do."

This time she studied him.

"I can give you references in Denver," he offered.

Lori couldn't help but be curious. Her life had been

exposed, yet she knew nothing about him. "Why did you leave there? Denver."

"Divorce. I had to sell the business to divide the joint assets. Moving here was my best chance to make a good home for my daughter. Best chance at getting full custody."

She might not like the man's bad attitude toward her, but wanting to be a good father gave him a lot of points.

"Once I finish Mountain Heritage and the spaces are leased, I'll have some revenue coming in. It'll allow me to control my work hours. I can pick and choose construction jobs so I can spend more time with Cassie." His gaze met hers. "Best of all, Destiny is a great place to raise children."

She smiled. "That I remember about this town, and how they decorated at Christmas."

She watched conflict play across his face. "That's what I want Cassie to experience, too. I don't want her in some boarding school in Europe because her mother doesn't have time for her." He stood, and quickly changed the subject. "I also have several men that are depending on this job."

"I need to talk to my lawyer before I can make any decision." And she needed to speak to Gina. Her sister weighed heavily in this decision. She turned toward Jace. "I know you were hoping for more."

He nodded. "Of course I was, but I can't wait much longer. Just so you know, I'll be contacting my own lawyer. I have to protect my investment."

Lori tried not to act surprised as she nodded. Jace Yeager finally said his goodbye as he stepped off the porch and walked around the house to the driveway.

She heard his truck start up. Just one more problem to deal with.

"Thanks, Dad." She glanced skyward. "You couldn't give me the time of day when you were alive, but now that you're gone, you turn my life upside down."

She walked back inside the house and back into her father's office. Paige and Mr. Bradley had their heads together. They spent the next twenty minutes going over all the details. She could contest the will, but if she lost, she'd lose everything and so would this town.

Mr. Bradley checked his watch, gathered up his papers and put them in his briefcase. "Lorelei, if you need anything else from me, just call." He handed her a business card. "There's one other thing I didn't get a chance to tell you. You only have seventy-two hours to make your decision," he said then walked out the door.

Lori looked at Paige. "How can I make a life-changing decision in three days?"

"I know it's difficult, Lori, but there isn't a choice. What can I say? Lyle liked being in control." The brunette smiled. "Sorry, I hate to speak ill of the dead."

"No need to apologize. Over the years, my mother never had anything nice to say about the man. It doesn't seem as if he ever changed."

She thought about what Lyle had done to Jace Yeager. The man would lose everything he'd invested in this project if he couldn't complete it. She closed her eyes. "What should I do?"

"Are you asking me as your lawyer or as a citizen of Destiny?"

"Both."

"As your lawyer, if you turn down Lyle's bequest, the corporation and the partnerships would be dissolved and all moneys would be given to charity. You'd get nothing, Lori." Paige went on to add, "As a citizen of a town I love, I hope you accept. Hutchinson Corporation employs many of the people in this community."

She groaned. "Lyle really did own this town."

Paige shrugged. "A fair share of it. But remember, the Hutchinsons built this town with the money they got from mining." She smiled. "Times are changing, though. My brother-in-law Justin is moving at a pretty good pace to take that status. He has an extreme skiing business. And don't count out Jace Yeager. He's got some other projects in the works."

"And now he's tied up in this mess," Lori said. "Dear Lord, you all must have hated my father."

"Like I said there's always been a Hutchinson here to deal with. Your grandfather Billy was a piece of work, too. He'd done a few shady deals in his time. The family has done a lot of good for Destiny." She tried not to smile. "Maybe Lyle was a little arrogant about it."

"And now it looks like you all have me to continue the tradition."

Paige raised an eyebrow. "Does that mean you're staying?"

"Do I have a choice?" She knew it was all about Lyle protecting the Hutchinsons' legacy. Not about his daughter's needs or wants. He had never cared about that.

Well, she had to think about what was best for her family. She and Gina had planned to move away from Colorado, and her sister's ex-husband. Most important they had to be safe. Could Eric find them here in Destiny? Would he try? Of course he would if he had any idea where to look.

If Lori decided to stay, at least she could afford to hire a bodyguard. "I need to talk to my sister. She would have to move here, too."

Paige nodded. "I understand. So when you make your decision give me a call anytime. I need to get back to the office." Her lawyer walked out, leaving her alone.

Lori went to the desk, sat down and opened the file. She stared once again at the exorbitant amount of money her father was worth. Although she was far from comfortable taking anything from Lyle, how could she walk away from this? The money would help her sister and nephew so much. Not to mention the other people in Destiny.

But she'd have to be able to work with Jace Yeager, too. The man had his own anger issues when it came to a Hutchinson. Could she handle that, or him? No, she doubted any woman could, but if she stayed out of his way, they might be able to be partners.

She took her cell phone from her purse and punched in the familiar number. When Gina answered, she said, "How would you feel about moving into a big house in Destiny?"

The next morning, Jace took his daughter to school then drove to the site. He needed to do everything he could to save this project. That meant convince Lori Hutchinson to stay. And that was what he planned to do.

He unlocked the chain-link fence that surrounded the deserted construction site. After opening the gate, he climbed back into his truck, pulled inside and parked in front of the two-story structure. The outside was nearly completed, except for some facade work.

Yet, inside was a different story. The loft apartments

upstairs were still only framed in and the same with the retail stores/office spaces on the bottom floor. He got out as the cool wind caused him to shove his cowboy hat down on his head. Checking the sky overhead, he could feel the moisture in the air. They were predicting rain for later today. How soon before it turned to snow? He'd seen it snow in October, in Colorado.

He heard a car and looked toward the dirt road to see Lori pull in next to his truck and get out. Though tall and slender, she still didn't reach his chin. He glanced down at her booted feet, then did a slow gaze over those long legs encased in a pair of worn jeans. Even in the cold air, his body took notice.

Calm down, boy. She was off-limits.

His gaze shot to her face. "Good morning. Welcome to Mountain Heritage."

"Morning," Lori returned as she burrowed deeper in her coat. "I hope this tour is going to be on the inside," she said. "It's really cold."

He nodded. "Come on."

He led her along the makeshift path through the maze of building materials to the entry. He'd been surprised when he'd gotten the call last night from her, saying she wanted to see Mountain Heritage.

"As you can see, the outside is nearly completed, just a little work left on the trim." He unlocked the door, and let her inside.

"We're ready to blow in insulation and hang Sheetrock. The electricians have completed the rough wiring." He glanced at her, but couldn't read anything from her expression. "This is going to be a green building, totally energy efficient, from the solar panels on the roof, to the tankless water heaters. Best of all, the outside of the structure blends in with the surrounding buildings. But this complex will offer so much more."

He pushed open the double doors and allowed her to go in first. He followed as she walked into the main lobby. This was where it all looked so different. The open concept was what he loved the most about the business complex. He'd done most of the design himself and was proud of how well it was turning out.

The framework of a winding staircase to the second-story balcony still needed the wooden banister. He motioned for her to follow him across the subfloor to the back hall, finding the elevators. He explained about the hardwood floors and the large stone fireplace.

"It's so large."

"We need the space to entice our clients. These back elevators lead to the ten loft apartments upstairs. Both Lyle and I figured they'd rent pretty well to the winter skiers. Of course our ideal renter would be long-term. We were hoping to make it a great place to live, shop and dine all without leaving the premises.

"We have a tentative agreement to lease office spaces for a ski rental company from Justin Hilliard. He's planning on doing a line of custom skis and snowboards."

"How soon were you supposed to have this all completed?"

Was she going to stay? "We'd been on schedule for the end of November." Now he was hoping he still had a full crew. Some of the subcontractors he'd been working with had come up from Durango.

Lori felt ignorant. She'd never been to a construction site. Doubts filled her again as she wondered for the hundredth time if she'd be any good taking over for

Lyle. So many people were depending on her. "How are you at teaching, Jace?"

He looked confused, then said, "I guess that depends on the student and how willing they are to learn."

"She's very serious." She released a sigh. "It looks like we're going to be partners."

Damn. Jace had a woman for his partner, a woman who didn't know squat about construction. And he was even taking her to lunch. He'd do whatever it took to provide for his daughter.

He escorted Lori into a booth at the local coffee shop, the Silver Spoon. He hadn't expected her to accept his lunch invitation, but they'd spent the past two hours at the site, going over everything that would need to happen in the next seven weeks to meet completion. She took notes, a lot of notes.

He'd made a call to his project manager, Toby Edwards, and had asked him to get together a crew. Within an hour, his foreman had called back to tell him they got most of the people on board to start first thing in the morning.

So it seemed natural that he would take her to lunch to celebrate. He glanced across the table. She still looked a little shell-shocked from all the information she'd consumed this morning, but she hadn't complained once.

"This place is nice, homey," she said. "Reminds me of the café I worked in during college."

Okay, that surprised him. "It's your typical family-run restaurant that serves good home cooking, a hearty breakfast in the morning and steak for supper. Outside of a steak house, there isn't any fine dining in Destiny, and Durango is forty-eight miles away. We're hoping a restaurant will be added to our complex. Not only more revenue for us, but more choice when you want to go out."

He smiled and Lori felt a sudden rush go through her. No. No. No. She didn't want to think about Jace Yeager being a man. Well, he was a man, just not the man she needed to be interested in. He was far too handsome, too distracting, and they would be working together. Correction, he was doing the work, she would be watching…and learning.

"I hear from your daughter that you've been remodeling your house."

"Restoration," he corrected. "And yes, it's a lot of work, but I enjoy it. So many people just want to tear out and put in new. There is so much you can save. I'm refinishing the hardwood floors, and stripping the crown moldings and the built-in cabinet in the dining room. What I've replaced is an outdated furnace and water heater."

She smiled. "And the roof?"

He raised an eyebrow.

She went on to say, "Cassie told me that you had to put out pans when it rained."

She caught a hint of his smile, making him even more handsome. "Yeah, we had a few adventurous nights. We stayed dry, though."

She couldn't help but be curious about him, but no more personal questions. Focus on his profession. "I bet my father's house could use some updating, too."

"I wouldn't know. Yesterday was the first time I'd been there. I conducted all my business with Lyle in his office at the bank."

She didn't get the chance to comment as the middle-aged waitress came to the table carrying two mugs and a coffeepot. With their nods, she filled the cups.

"Hi, Jace. How's that little one of yours?"

"She keeps me on my toes." He smiled. "Helen, this is Lorelei Hutchinson. Lori, this is Helen Turner. She and her husband, Alan, are the owners of the Silver Spoon."

The woman smiled. "It's nice to meet you, Ms. Hutchinson. I'm sorry about your father."

"Thank you. And please, call me Lori."

"Will you be staying in town long?" the woman asked.

Lori glanced at Jace. "It looks that way."

She couldn't tell if Helen was happy about that or not. They placed their order and the woman walked away.

"I guess she hasn't decided if she's happy about me staying."

Jace leaned forward. "Everyone is curious about what you're going to do. Whether you'll change things at Hutchinson Corp." He shrugged. "These days everyone worries about their jobs."

"I don't want that to happen. That's one of the main reasons I'm staying in town."

Jace leaned back in the booth. "Of course it has nothing to do with the millions your father left you."

Lori felt the shock. "Money doesn't solve every problem."

"My ex-wife thought it did."

Before she could react to Jace's bitter words, Helen brought their food to the table. Their focus turned to their meal until a middle-aged man approached their booth.

"Excuse me, ma'am, sir," he began hesitantly. "Helen told me that you're Mr. Hutchinson's daughter."

Lori smiled. "I am Lori Hutchinson and you are…?"

"Mac Burleson."

She had a feeling that he wasn't just here to be neighborly. Had her father done something to him? "It's nice to meet you, Mr. Burleson."

Mr. Burleson looked to be in his early thirties. Dressed in faded jeans, a denim shirt and warm winter jacket, he held his battered cowboy hat in his hands. "I hope you'll pardon the intrusion, ma'am, but your father and I had business before his death. First, I'm sorry for your loss."

She nodded. "Thank you."

"I was also wondering if you'll be taking over his position at the bank."

She was startled by the question. "To be honest with you, Mr. Burleson, I haven't had much chance to decide what my involvement would be. Is there a problem?"

The man was nervous. "It's just that, Mr. Neal, in the loan department, is going to foreclose on my house next week." The man glanced at Jace, then back at her.

"I know I've been late on my payments, but I haven't been able to find work in a while. No one is hiring…." He stopped and gathered his emotions. "I have three kids, Miss Hutchinson. If I can have a little more time, I swear I'll catch up. Just don't make my family leave their home."

Lori was caught off guard. Her father planned to evict a family?

"Mac," Jace said, drawing the man's attention, "do you have any experience working construction?"

Hope lit up the man's tired eyes. "I've worked on a

few crews. I can hang drywall and do rough framing. Heck, I'll even clean up trash." He swallowed hard. "I'm not too proud to do anything to feed my family."

Lori felt an ache building in her stomach as Jace talked. "If you can report to the Mountain Heritage site tomorrow morning at seven, I'll give you a chance to prove yourself."

"I'll be there," Mac promised. "Thank you."

Jace nodded. "Report to the foreman, Toby."

Mac shook Jace's hand. "I won't let you down, Mr. Yeager." He turned back to Lori. "Could you tell Mr. Neal that I have a job now? And maybe give me a few months to catch up on my payments."

Lori's heart ached. She didn't even know her loan officer, but it seemed she needed to meet him right away. "Mac, I can't make any promises, but give me a few days and I'll get back to you."

He shook her hand. "That's all I can ask. Thank you, Ms. Hutchinson." He walked away.

Lori released a sigh. "I guess I have a lot more to do now than worry about one building."

"Your job as Hutchinson CEO covers a lot of areas."

Helen came over to the table, this time wearing a grin.

"I hoped you've enjoyed your lunch."

"Great as usual," Jace said.

The waitress started to turn away, then stopped and said, "By the way, it's on the house." She picked up the bill from the table. "Thank you both for what you did for Mac."

"I haven't done anything yet," Lori clarified, now afraid she'd spoken too soon.

"You both gave him hope. He's had a rough time of

late." Helen blinked. "A few years ago, he left the army and came back home a decorated war hero. At the very least, he deserves our respect, and a chance. So thank you for taking the time to listen to him." The woman turned and walked back toward the kitchen.

She looked at Jace, remembering what he said about her inheritance. She also wasn't sure she liked being compared to his ex. "I better go and stop by the bank." She pushed her plate away. "Who knows, maybe all those 'millions' just might do some good."

CHAPTER FOUR

LORI couldn't decide if she was hurt or angry over Jace's assumption about the inheritance. She'd lost her appetite and excused herself immediately after lunch.

She was glad when he didn't try to stop her, because she had a lot of thinking to do without the opinion of a man she'd be working with. And who seemed to have a lot of issues about women.

Was he like her father? What she'd learned from her mother about Lyle over the years had been his need to control, whether in business or his personal life. When Jocelyn Hutchinson couldn't take any more she'd gotten out of the marriage, but their child had still been trapped in the middle of her parents' feud. The scars they'd caused made it hard for Lori to trust.

But was coming back to Destiny worth putting her smack-dab into dealing with the past? All the childhood hurt and pain? It also put her in charge of Lyle's domain, and his business dealings, including the Mountain Heritage complex. And a lot more time with the handsome but irritating Jace Yeager.

The man had been right about something. She had a lot of money and it could do a lot of good. She recalled the look of hope on Mac Burleson's face and knew she needed to find an answer for the man.

She crossed the street to Destiny Community Bank. The two-story brick structure was probably from her grandfather's era. With renewed confidence she walked inside to a large open space with four teller windows. Along the wall were portraits of generations of the Hutchinson men—Raymond, William, Billy and Lyle. They were all strangers to her. She studied her hand-some father's picture. This man especially.

She turned around and found several of the bank customers watching her. She put on a smile and they greeted her the same way as if they knew who she was.

She went to the reception desk and spoke to the young brunette woman seated there. "Is it possible to see Mr. Neal? Tell him Lorelei Hutchinson is here."

"Yes, Miss Hutchinson." The woman picked up the phone, and when she hung up said, "Mr. Neal said to have a seat and he'll be out…shortly."

Lori wasn't in the mood to wait. "Is he in a meeting?"

The girl shook her head.

"Then I'll just head to his office. Where is it?"

The receptionist stood and together they went toward a row of offices. "Actually, he's in Mr. Hutchinson's office."

Lori smiled. "Oh, is he? Excuse me, I didn't get your name."

"It's Erin Peters."

"Well, Erin, it's very nice to meet you. I'm Lori." She stuck out her hand. "Have you worked at the bank for long?"

"Three years. I've been taking college classes for my business degree."

"That's nice to know. I'm sure my father appreciated his employees continuing their education."

Erin only nodded as they walked toward the office at the end of the hall. Lori knocked right under the name-plate on the last door that read Lyle W. Hutchinson. She paused as she gathered courage, then turned the knob and walked in.

There was a balding man of about fifty seated behind her father's desk. He seemed busy trying to stack folders. When he saw her he froze, then quickly put on a smile.

"Well, you must be Lorelei Hutchinson." He rounded the desk. "I'm Gary Neal. It's a pleasure to finally meet you. Lyle talked about you often."

She shook his hand, seriously doubting Lyle said much about her. Her father hadn't taken the time to know her. Now, did she have to prove herself worthy of being his daughter?

"Hello, Mr. Neal."

"First off, I want to express my deepest sympathies for your loss. Lyle and I were not only colleagues, but friends. So if there is anything you need…"

"Thank you, I'm fine." She nodded. "I've only been in town a few days, but I wanted to stop by the bank. I'm sure you've already heard that I'm going to be staying in Destiny."

He nodded. "Dennis Bradley explained as much."

She hesitated. "Good. Do you have a few minutes to talk with me?"

"Of course."

Still feeling brave, she walked behind the desk and took the seat in her father's chair as if she belonged.

She didn't miss the surprise on the loan officer's face. "Where's your office, Mr. Neal?"

He blinked, then finally said, "It's two doors down the hall. Since your father's death, I've had to access some files from here. Lyle was hands-on when it came to bank business. I'm his assistant manager."

"Good. Then you're who I need to speak with." She motioned for him to sit down, but she was feeling a little shaky trying to pull this off. This man could be perfectly wonderful at his job, but she needed to trust him. "I take it you handle the mortgage loans." With his nod, she asked, "What do you know about the Mac Burleson mortgage?"

The man frowned. "Funny you should ask, I was just working on the Burleson file."

"Could I have a look?"

He hesitated, then relented. "It's a shame we're going to have to start foreclosure proceedings in a few days."

Neal dug through the stack, located the file and handed it to her. She looked over pages of delinquent notices, the huge late fees. And an interest rate that was nearly three points higher than the norm. No wonder the man was six months behind. "Has Mr. Burleson paid anything during all this time?"

"Yes, but it could barely cover the interest."

"Why didn't you help him by dropping the interest rate and lowering the payments?"

"It's not the bank's policy. Your father—"

"Well, my father is gone now, and he wanted me to take over in his place."

"I'm *sure* he did, but with your limited experience…"

"That may be, but I feel that given the state of the economy we need to help people, too. It's a rough time."

She knew firsthand. "I want to stop the foreclosure, or at least delay it."

"But Mr. Burleson isn't even employed."

"As of an hour ago, he's gotten a job offer." She looked at the remaining eight files. "Are these other homes to be foreclosed on, too?"

The loan officer looked reluctant to answer, but nodded. "Would you please halt all proceedings until I have a look at each case? I want to try everything to keep these families in their homes." She stood. "Maybe if we can set up a meeting next week and see what we can come up with."

Mr. Neal stood. "This isn't bank policy. If people aren't held accountable for their debts, we'd be out of business. I'm sure your father wouldn't agree with this, either."

For the first time in days, Lori felt as if she were doing the right thing. "As I said before, my father left me in charge. Do you have a problem with that, Mr. Neal?"

With the shaking of his head, she tossed out one more request. "Good. I also need money transferred into the escrow account for the Mountain Heritage project as soon as possible. Mr. Yeager will have his crew back to work first thing in the morning. And if you have any questions about my position here, talk to Mr. Bradley."

She walked out to the reception desk and found Jace standing there, talking with Erin. He was smiling at the pretty brunette woman. Why not? He was handsome and single. And why did she even care?

He finally saw her and walked over. "Hi, Lori."

"What are you doing here? I told you that I'd get the money for the project."

"I know you did, but that's not why I'm here—"

"I'm really busy now, Jace. Could we do this later?" She cut him off and turned to the receptionist. "Erin, would you schedule a meeting for all employees for nine o'clock tomorrow in the conference room?"

With Erin's agreement, Lori walked out of the bank, feeling Jace's gaze on her. She couldn't deal with him. She had more pressing things to do, like moving out of the inn and into her father's house, where she had to face more ghosts.

Jace was angry that he let Lori get to him. He'd wasted his afternoon chasing after a woman who didn't want to be found. At least not by him.

He hadn't blamed Lori for walking out on him at lunch. Okay, maybe he had no right to say what he did to her. Damn. He'd let his past dictate his feelings about women. Like it or not, Lori Hutchinson was his partner. More importantly, she had the money to keep the project going. If he wanted any chance of keeping Cassie he had to complete his job.

An apology was due to Lori. And he needed to deliver it in person. If only she'd give him a minute to listen to him. He also needed her to sign some papers that needed her authorization.

Jace left the bank to meet up with his foreman to finalize the crew for tomorrow. Then the search for Lori continued as he'd gone around town and ended up at the inn, where he finally got an answer as to her whereabouts.

He had to pick up Cassie from school, but went straight to the Hutchinson house after. He drove through the gates, hoping he could come up with something to say to her. The last thing he wanted was to start off on the wrong foot.

"Wow! Daddy, this is pretty. Does Ms. Lori really live here?"

He parked in the driveway and saw the rental car there. "Yes, she does. It was her father's, now it's hers."

He climbed out and helped Cassie from the back-seat. They went up the steps as the front door opened and Maggie appeared. "This is a wonderful day. First, Ms. Lorelei comes home and now, Mr. Yeager and this beautiful child come to visit."

"Hi, Maggie," Jace said. "This is my daughter, Cassie. Cassie, this is Maggie."

They exchanged greetings then the housekeeper opened the door wider.

"I'd like to see Lori if she isn't too busy."

"Of course." Maggie motioned them inside the entry. "She's in her father's upstairs office." The housekeeper looked at Cassie. "Why don't I take you into the kitchen and see if there are some fresh baked cookies on my cooling rack? They're so good along with some milk." The housekeeper looked concerned. "Coming back here is hard for her."

"I expect it is. Are you sure it's okay?"

Maggie smiled. "I think that would be good. The office is the first door on the left."

Still he hesitated.

"You should go up," the woman said. "She could use a friend right about now."

Jace glanced up the curved staircase and murmured, "I'm not sure she'd call me 'friend' right now."

* * *

Lori had trouble deciding where to put her things. There were six bedrooms and a master suite. One had been turned into an office, and the one next to it was nondescript, with only a queen-size bed covered by a soft floral comforter. It had a connecting bath, so that was where she put her one bag.

She unpacked the few items she had, but went into her father's office. She couldn't get into his computer because she didn't have access.

"Okay, need to make a call to Dennis Bradley first thing tomorrow."

What she knew for sure was she needed to have someone to work with. Someone she trusted. As far as she knew her father had worked out of his office at the bank and from home. Did Lyle handle everything himself? Had he not trusted anyone? She rubbed her hands over her face. She didn't know the man. She stood up and walked out.

In the hall curiosity got the best of her and she began to look around. She peeked into the next room, then the next until she came to the master suite. She opened the door but didn't go inside.

The dark room had a big four-poster bed that dominated the space. The windows were covered with heavy brocade drapes and the bedspread was the same fabric. The furniture was also stained dark. Bits and pieces of childhood memories hit her. She pushed them aside and journeyed on to the next room. She paused at the door, feeling a little shaky, then she turned the knob and pushed it open.

She gasped, seeing the familiar pale pink walls. The double bed with the sheer white canopy and matching sheer curtains. There was a miniature table with stuffed animals seated in the matching chairs as if waiting for a tea party.

Oh, my God.

Nothing had been changed since she'd lived here. Lori crossed the room to the bed where a brown teddy bear was propped against the pillow.

"Buddy?" She picked up the furry toy, feeling a rush of emotions, along with the memory of her father bringing the stuffed animal home one night.

She hugged the bear close and fought tears. No, she didn't want to feel like this. She didn't want to care about the man who didn't want her. Yet, she couldn't stop the flood of tears. A sob tore from her throat as she sank down onto the mattress and cried.

"Lori?"

She heard Jace's voice and stiffened. She quickly walked to the window, wiping her eyes. She fought to compose herself before she had to face him.

He followed her, refusing to be ignored.

"It's okay to be sad," he said, his voice husky and soft.

She finally swung around. "Don't talk about what you know nothing about."

Jace was taken aback by her anger. "It seems that everything I've said to you today has been wrong. I won't bother you again."

She stopped him. "No, please, don't go."

She wiped the last of the tears off her face. "It's me who should apologize for my rudeness. You caught me at a bad moment. Why are you here?"

"Maggie sent me up to Lyle's office. I have some papers for you to sign, but they can wait. Believe it or not, Lori, I came to apologize for what I said to you at lunch. I had no right to judge your motivation."

Jace glanced around the bedroom and hated what he was feeling. What Lyle must have felt when his daughter left. Would this happen to him if his ex got Cassie back? "I take it you were about six or seven when you left here?"

She nodded. "It was so long ago, I feel silly for letting it upset me now."

"You were old enough to have memories. Your childhood affects you all your life. It was your father who chose not to spend time with you." It seemed odd, he thought, because Lyle had kept her room like a shrine.

Lori suddenly brightened as if all the pain went away. "Well, as you can see, I'll need to do some painting. My sister, Gina, is coming soon along with my nephew, Zack." She put on a smile. "I don't think he'd like a pink bedroom."

Before Jace could say anything, he heard his daughter calling for him. "I'm in here, Cassie. I picked her up from school, and I wanted to see you before work tomorrow. To make sure everything is okay…between us."

The expression on his seven-year-old's face was priceless as she stopped at the door. "Oh, it's so pretty." She looked at Lori. "Do you have a little girl, too?"

An hour later, with Cassie busy doing homework at the kitchen table, Jace and Lori went to do their work in Lyle's office.

"I hate that you have to keep going over everything again and again," Lori told him.

"It's not a problem. Better now, when I'm around to answer your questions. There aren't too many decisions to make right now. If you'd like to put in some input on finishes, like tile and countertops, you're more than welcome. A woman's touch." He held up a hand. "I didn't mean anything about that. A second opinion would be nice."

"I'd like that."

She smiled and he felt a tightening in his gut. Damn. He looked back at the work sheet.

"Well, the crew is showing up tomorrow to start the finish work on the outside. If we're lucky the weather will hold and we can complete everything before the snow comes."

"Will it affect the work inside?"

"Only if we can't get the materials to the site because the roads aren't passable."

She nodded, chewing her bottom lip. He found it hard to look away.

"What about Mac Burleson? Do you really have a job for him?"

Jace nodded. "If he can do the work."

"I wonder if Mac can paint," Lori said.

Jace looked at her to see a mischievous grin on her pretty face. She wasn't beautiful as much as striking. Those sparkling brown eyes and full mouth… "That was probably going to be one of his jobs—priming the walls once they're up. What were you thinking?"

"I doubt my father has done much work on this house in years." She shrugged. "I don't mind so much for myself, but Gina and Zack. I want this place…" She glanced around the dark room. "A little more homey. I want to talk to Charlie and see what he has to say about repairs."

"How soon are you expecting your family?"

"Next week. Gina is packing and putting most of the furniture in storage." She sighed. "I should go back to help her, but I want to make sure there won't be any holdup on the project."

Jace needed to remember that her entire life had been turned upside down by Lyle's death. "It's a shame you have to leave everything behind, like your friends. A boyfriend…?"

She looked surprised at his question. Not as much as he was. He stood and went to the window. "I only meant, Lyle had you make a tough choice."

"No, I don't have a boyfriend at the moment, and my sister is my best friend. So sometimes a fresh start is good." She turned the tables on him. "Isn't that why you came to Destiny?"

He didn't look at her, but that didn't mean he couldn't catch her scent, or wasn't aware of her closeness. He took a step back. "I came here to make a life for my daughter. She's everything to me."

Lori smiled at him and again his body took notice. "From what I've seen, Cassie feels the same way about you. You're a good father."

"Thank you. I'm not perfect. But I do try and want to make the job permanent."

His gaze went back to her. Darn. What was it about her that drew him? Suddenly he thought about his ex-wife, and the caution flag came out. He needed to stay focused on two things—business and his daughter.

A happy Cassie skipped into the room and rushed to him. "Maggie said to tell you that dinner is ready."

"Oh, honey. We should head home." He glanced at his watch. "Maybe another time."

"No, Daddy. We can't go. I helped Maggie make the biscuits, so we have to stay and eat them."

He was caught as he looked down at his daughter, then at Lori.

"I can't believe you're passing up a home-cooked meal, Jace Yeager," Lori said. "Maggie's biscuits are the best around, and probably even better with Cassie helping."

"Please, Daddy. I'll go to bed right on time. I won't argue or anything."

Jace looked back at Lori. It was her first night here, and would probably be a rough one.

Lori smiled. "Now that's a hard offer to turn down."

"You're no help," he told Lori.

"Sorry, us girls have to stick together."

That was what he was afraid of. He was losing more than just this round. He hated that he didn't mind one bit.

"Okay, but we can't stay long. We have a bedtime schedule."

"I promise, I'll go to bed right on time," Cassie said, then took off toward the kitchen.

He looked at a smiling Lori. "Okay, I'm a pushover."

"Buck up, Dad. It's only going to get worse before it gets better."

Suddenly their eyes locked and the amused look disappeared. Lori was the first to speak. "Please, I want you to stay for dinner. I think we both agree that eating alone isn't fun."

"Yes, we can agree on that."

He followed Lori into the kitchen, knowing this

woman could easily fill those lonely times. He just couldn't let that happen. No more women for a while, at least not over the age of seven.

CHAPTER FIVE

AT EIGHT-THIRTY the next morning, Lori was up and dressed, and grabbed a travel mug of coffee from Maggie, then she was out the door to the construction site. Not that she didn't think Jace could do his job, but she wanted to meet the crew and assure them that there wouldn't be any more delays with the project.

When she pulled through the gate and saw the buzz of activity, she was suddenly concerned about disturbing everyone.

She had every right to be here, she thought as she climbed out of her car and watched the men working on the trim work of the two-story structure. Jace hadn't wasted any time.

She walked carefully on the soggy ground. Okay, she needed more protection than her loafers. A good pair of sturdy boots was on her list. She headed up the plywood-covered path when a young man dressed in jeans, a denim work shirt and lace-up steel-toed boots came toward her.

He gave her a big smile and tipped back his hard hat. "Can I help you, ma'am?"

"I'm looking for Jace Yeager."

The man's smile grew bigger. "Aren't they all? I'm Mike Parker, maybe I can help you."

All? Lori couldn't help but wonder what that meant. She started to speak when she heard a familiar voice call out. They both turned to see Jace. He was dressed pretty much like the others, but he had on a leather vest over a black Henley shirt even though the temperature was in the low fifties.

Lori froze as he gave her a once-over. He didn't look happy to see her as he made his way toward them.

Jace ignored her as he looked at Mike. "Don't you have anything to do?"

"I was headed to my truck for some tools." He nodded to her. "And I ran across this nice lady. Sorry, I didn't catch your name."

"Lori Hutchinson."

Mike let out a low whistle. "So you're the big boss? I can't tell you how good it is to meet you, Ms. Hutchinson."

She tried not to cringe at the description. "It's Lori. I'm not anyone's boss. Jace is in charge of this project."

That was when Jace spoke up. "Mike, they've finished spraying the insulation up in the lofts, so I need you to get started hanging drywall."

"Right, I'll get on it." He tipped his hat to Lori. "Nice to meet you, ma'am."

"Nice to meet you, too, Mike."

She watched him hurry off, then turned back to Jace. "Good morning. Seems you've been busy. What time did you start?"

"I had a partial crew in at five."

"What about Cassie?"

He seemed surprised at her question. "I wasn't here,

but my foreman was. My daughter comes first, Lori. She always will."

"I didn't mean… I apologize."

That didn't ease the scowl on his face. "Were we supposed to meet this morning?"

She shook her head. "No."

"Did you come to work?" He looked over her attire. "You're not exactly dressed for a construction site."

She glanced down at her dark trousers and soft blue sweater under her coat. "I have an appointment at the bank later this morning. I wanted to stop here first to see if everything got off okay. Do you need anything?"

"No, it's fine. I know it looks a little chaotic, but things are running pretty smoothly for the first day back to work. It's most of the same crew so they know what I expect from them."

Lori had no doubt that Jace Yeager was good at his job. "So everything is on schedule?"

"If the weather holds." The wind picked up and brushed her hair back. "Come inside where it's a little warmer," he said. "I'll introduce you to the foreman."

"I don't want to disturb him."

"As you can see, it's a little late for that." He nodded toward the men who were watching.

She could feel a blush rising over her face as she followed Jace inside the building to a worktable that had blueprints spread out on top. A middle-aged man was talking with another workman.

"Hey, Toby," Jace called as he reached into a bin and pulled out a hard hat. He came to her and placed it on her head. "You need to wear this if you come here. Safety rules."

Their eyes met. "Thank you."

Toby walked up to them. "What, Jace?"

"This is Lori Hutchinson. Lori, this is my foreman, Toby Edwards."

The man smiled at her and tiny lines crinkled around his eyes. "So you're the one who saved this guy's as… sets."

Lori felt Jace tense. "I'd say I was just lucky to inherit some money," she told Toby. "Speaking of money…" She turned to Jace. "Were the funds transferred into the Mountain Heritage account?"

He nodded. "Yes. We're expecting materials to be delivered later today."

"Good." She glanced around, feeling a little excited about being a part of this. "It's nice to see all the work going on." It was a little noisy with the saws and nail guns.

Jace watched Lori. He wasn't expecting her here. Not that she didn't have a right, but she was a big distraction. He caught the guys watching her, too. Okay, they were curious about their attractive new boss. He hoped that was all it was. There could be a problem if she stopped by every day. And not only for his men, either. He eyed her pretty face and those big brown eyes that a man could get lost in.

No way. One woman had already cost him his career and future, and maybe his daughter. He wasn't going to get involved with another, especially in his workplace. Or any other place. He thought about the cozy dinner last night in the Hutchinson kitchen.

It was a little too cozy.

Enough reminiscing, he thought, and stuck his fingers in his mouth, letting go with a piercing whistle. "Let's get this over with so we can all get on with our day." All work stopped and the men came to the center of the main room.

"Everyone, this is Lorelei Hutchinson. Since Lyle Hutchinson's death, Lori will be taking over in her father's place. It's thanks to her we're all back to work on this project." The men let go with cheers and whistles. Jace forced a smile, knowing this was a means to get this project completed. But damn, being beholden to a woman stuck in his craw. "Okay, now back to work."

"Thank you," Lori said. "So many people in town have been looking at me like I have two heads."

"Has someone said anything to you?" he asked.

"No, but they're wondering what I'm going to do." She shrugged. "Maybe I should just make a big announcement in the town square. 'Hey, everyone, I'm not here to cause trouble.'"

A strange protective feeling came over him. "Now that the project has started up again, maybe they'll stop worrying."

"I hope so. I'm bringing my sister and nephew here to live. I want to be part of this community."

"What you did for Mac Burleson yesterday was a pretty good start."

"Oh, Mac. Is he here?"

Jace nodded. "Yeah, he was here waiting when Toby opened the gates."

She glanced around the area. "How is he doing?"

"Good so far."

She looked up at Jace. "There he is. Would you mind if I talked to him for a moment?"

"No, not a problem."

She walked across the large entry to the wall. Jace watched her acknowledge a lot of the workers before she got to Mac. She smiled and the man returned it. In fact he was smiling the whole time Lori was talking. Then he shook her hand and Lori walked back. "I just hired Mac to paint a couple of bedrooms at the house."

"Hey, are you stealing my help?"

"No. He's agreed to come over this weekend with his brother and paint the upstairs. I don't think my nephew wants to sleep in a pink room."

Jace nodded, knowing she would be erasing the last of her own memories of her childhood. "There are other bedrooms for him to sleep in."

"I know, but it should have been changed years ago."

"Maybe there was a reason why it hadn't been."

She looked at him. He saw pain, but also hope. "Lyle Hutchinson knew where I was since I left here twenty-two years ago. My father could have invited me back anytime. He chose not to."

Lori turned to walk out and he hurried to catch up with her. "Look, Lori. I don't know the situation."

She stopped abruptly. "That's right, you don't." She closed her eyes. "Look, it was a long time ago. My father is gone, and I'll never know why he never came to see me. And now, why in heaven's name does he want me to run his company?"

"I can't answer that, either."

"I've dealt with it. So now I move on and start my new life with Gina and Zack. I want them to have a fresh start here, in a new place, a new house and especially a new bedroom for my seven-year-old nephew."

Jace frowned. "I take it Zack is without his father."

Lori straightened. "His parents are divorced." She glanced around. "I should be going."

"I need to get back, too."

They started walking toward the door. "If there's anything you need," she offered, "just give me a call. You have my cell phone number. I'll be at the bank most of today."

He walked her out. "I can handle things here." Then he felt bad. "Maybe in a few days if you're available we could go over some samples of tiles and flooring."

She looked surprised at his request. "I'd like that. I want to be a part of this project."

Her steps slowed as she made her way over the uneven boards. He took Lori's arm, helping her along the path.

"What about the bank?"

"I doubt Mr. Neal will enjoy having me around." She stopped suddenly and nearly lost her balance. "Oh," she gasped.

"I got you." He caught her in his arms. Suddenly her trim body was plastered up against him. Even with her coat he wasn't immune to her soft curves. And he liked it. Too much. He finally got her back on her feet. "You need practical boots if you come to a construction site. Go to Travers's Outfitters and get some that are waterproof. You don't want to be caught in bad weather without protection."

She stopped next to her compact car. "I need a lot of things since I'll be living here awhile."

"Like a car that will get through the snow. This thing will put you in a ditch on the first bad day. Get something with bulk to it. You'll be driving your family around."

She nodded. "I guess I need to head down to Durango and visit a dealership next week when my sister flies in."

Before he could stop himself, he offered, "If you need any help, let me know."

She gave him a surprised look, mirroring his own feelings.

Two hours later, Lori glanced across the conference table at the Destiny Community Bank's loan officers, Gary Neal, Harold Brownlee and Larry McClain. The gentlemen's club. "I disagree. In this day and age, we need to work with people and help adjust their loans."

"In my experience," Neal said, "if we start giving handouts, people will take advantage. And no one will pay us."

She tried to remain calm, but she was so far out of her element it wasn't funny.

"I never said this is a handout, more like a hand up. All I suggested is we lower the interest rates on these loans." She pointed to the eight mortgages. "Two points. Waive the late fees and penalties. Just give these families a fighting chance to keep their homes. We'll get the money we loaned back." She paused to see their stunned looks and wondered if she were crazy, too.

She hurried on to say, "Mac Burleson has a job now, but he can't catch up on his mortgage if we don't help him."

"We've always done things this way," Larry McClain said. "Your father would never—"

Lori stiffened. "Well, I'm not my father, but he did put me in charge. In fact, I'm going to become more involved in day-to-day working here at the bank. I can see that there aren't any women in management positions. That needs to change, too."

The threesome gave each other panicked looks. "That's not true. Mary O'Brien manages the tellers."

Were these men from the Dark Ages? "I mean women in decision-making positions. It's a changing world out there and we need to keep up. I've seen the profit sheet for this bank. Over the years, it's done very well."

Neal spoke up again. "You can't come in here and just change everything. You're a schoolteacher."

Lori held her temper. "I became an expert when my father put me in charge of his company. Just so you know, not only am I a good teacher, but I also minored in business. So, gentlemen, whether you like it or not, I'm here."

She was feeling a little shaky. What if she was making a mistake? She glanced at her watch. "I think we've said about everything that needs to be said for now. Good morning." She took her purse and walked out.

She needed someone here on her side. She walked to Erin's desk.

The girl smiled when she approached. "Hello, Ms. Hutchinson. How was your meeting?"

"Not as productive as I would have liked." She sat down in the chair next to the desk. "Erin, could you help me?"

The girl nodded. "If I can."

"I'm looking for someone, a woman who is qualified for a managerial position. Could you give me some candidates?"

The pretty brunette looked surprised, but then answered. "That would be Mary O'Brien and Lisa Kramer. They've both worked for the bank for over five years.

I know Lisa has a college degree. I'm not sure Mary does, but she practically runs this bank."

"That's good to know, because I need someone to help me." She was going to need a lot of help. Since her father had never promoted a woman that was one of the things she needed to change. Immediately.

"Could you call a meeting with all the employees?" She looked at her watch. "And call the Silver Spoon and have them send over sandwiches and drinks."

Erin smiled. "This is going to be fun."

"We're going to need our strength to get this bank into the twenty-first century."

Two mornings later, Lori had been awakened by a call from a sick Claire Keenan, asking her for a favor. Would Lori like to take her place as a volunteer in the second grade classroom this afternoon?

There might have been several other things to do, but Lori found she wanted to check out the school. After her trip to the paint store and picking her colors for the bedroom, she had her purchase sent to the house.

She grabbed a quick lunch at the Silver Spoon, and after a friendly chat with Helen, she arrived at Destiny Elementary with time to spare. She went through the office then was taken down the hall to the second grade classroom.

Outside, she was greeted by the teacher. "It's good to meet you, I'm Julie Miller."

"Lori Hutchinson. I'm substituting for Claire Keenan. She's sick."

The young strawberry blonde smiled eagerly. "I'm glad you could make it. I've heard a lot about you."

"Well, I guess Lyle's long-lost daughter would be news in a small town."

Julie smiled. "No, I heard it all from Cassie Yeager. Seems you live in a castle and have a princess bedroom like hers."

That brought a smile to Lori's lips, too. "If only."

"I also heard you teach second grade."

"I did. I was laid off this year."

"I'm sorry to hear that, but you're welcome to come and help out in my class anytime. But it sounds like you've been pretty busy with other projects around town."

Lori blinked. "You must have a good source."

"My sister, Erin, works at the bank. You've really impressed her."

"Oh, Erin. She's been a big help showing me around. There do need to be some changes."

Julie smiled brightly. "I can't tell you how happy I am that you came to Destiny and I hope you stay."

"I'll be here for this year anyway. In fact, my sister and her son will be coming in next week. Zack will be in second grade."

"That's wonderful. Then you'll want to see how I run my class."

Julie Miller opened the door to a room that was buzzing with about twenty-five seven-year-olds. The room was divided in sections, half with desks, the other half with tables and a circle of chairs for reading time.

Suddenly two little blonde girls came up to her—Ellie Larkin and Cassie Yeager.

"Miss Lori, what are you doing here?" Cassie asked.

"Hi, girls. Ellie, your grandmother isn't feeling well today."

Both girls looked worried. "Really?" Ellie said.

"It's nothing serious, don't worry. But she asked if I'd come in her place."

They got excited again. "We're going to try out for our Christmas program today."

"That's wonderful," Lori said. This was what she missed about teaching, the children's enthusiasm.

"It's called Destiny's First Christmas," Cassie said as she clasped her hands together. "And everyone gets to be in it."

"But we want to be the angels," Ellie added.

Just then Mrs. Miller got their attention. "Okay, class, you need to return to your desks. We have a special guest today and we need to show her how well-behaved we are so she'll want to come back." A bright smile. "Maybe Miss Hutchinson will help us with our Christmas play."

CHAPTER SIX

LATER that evening, Jace finally headed home. He was beat to say the least. A twelve-hour day was usually nothing for him, but he'd been off for three weeks. He needed to oversee everything today to make sure that the schedule for tomorrow went off without a hitch. The one thing he knew, he didn't like to be away from Cassie that long. Luckily, he had good childcare.

He came up the road and the welcoming two-story clapboard house came into view. Although the sun had set an hour ago, he had installed plenty of lighting to illuminate the grounds, including the small barn. He had a lot of work yet to do on the place, but a new roof and paint job made the house livable for now.

The barn had been redone, plus he'd added stalls for his two horses, Rocky and Dixie. Maybe it was a luxury he couldn't afford right now, but it was something that had helped Cassie adjust to her move. Luckily he'd been able to hire the neighbor's teenage son to do the feeding and cleaning.

Jace frowned at the sight of a new SUV parked by the back door. Had Heather, the babysitter, gotten a new car? Then dread washed over him. Was it his ex-wife?

Panic surged through him as he got out of his truck

and hurried up the back steps into the mudroom. After shucking his boots, he walked into the kitchen. He froze, then almost with relief, he sagged against the counter when he saw his daughter at the kitchen table with Lori Hutchinson.

He took a moment and watched the interaction of the two. Their blond heads together, working on the math paper. Then Lori reached out and stroked Cassie's hair and it looked as natural as if they were mother and daughter. His throat suddenly went dry. His business partner had a whole new side to her, a very appealing side.

Too appealing. Lorelei Hutchinson was beginning to be more than a business partner and a pretty face. She had him thinking about the things he'd always wanted in his life. In his daughter's life.

Cassie finally turned to him. "Daddy." She got up and rushed over to him. "You're home."

He hugged her, but his gaze was on Lori. "Yes, sorry I'm so late."

"It's okay," she said. "Miss Lori drove me home." His daughter gave him a bright smile. "She's helping me with my homework."

"I thought Mrs. Keenan was going to do that." He'd made the arrangements with her yesterday.

Lori stood. "Claire would have, but she got sick. I took over for her this afternoon in Cassie's classroom, and I offered to bring her home. I knew you would be busy at the site."

Jace tensed. "My daughter is a priority. I'm never too busy to be here for her. At the very least I should have been called." He glanced around for the teenager who he depended on. "Where's Heather?"

"She had a 'mergency at her house," Cassie told him.

He turned to the jean-clad Lori. She didn't look much older than the high school babysitter.

"We tried to call you but I got your voice mail," Lori said. "It wasn't a problem for me to stay with Cassie until you got home."

Jace felt the air go out of him, remembering he hadn't had his phone on him. He wasn't sure where it was at the site. He looked at Lori. "Thank you. I guess I got wrapped up in getting things back on target at the job site."

"It's okay, Daddy." His daughter looked up at him. "'Cause we made supper."

Great. All he needed was for this woman to get involved in his personal life. "You didn't need to do that."

Lori caught on pretty quickly that Jace didn't want her here. She'd gotten rejection before, so why had his bothered her so much?

"Look, it's just some potato soup and corn bread." She checked her watch. "Oh, my, it's late, I should go."

"No!" Cassie said. "You have to stay. You said you'd help me practice my part in the play." She turned back to her father. "Daddy, Miss Lori has to stay."

Lori hated to put Jace on the spot. Whatever the issues he had about women, she didn't want to know. She had enough to deal with. "It's okay, Cassie, we'll work on it another time."

"But Miss Lori, you wanted to show Daddy your new car, too."

Lori picked up her coat and was slipping it on when Jace came after her.

"Cassie's right, Lori. Please stay."

His husky voice stopped her, but those blue eyes convinced her to change her mind about leaving.

His voice lowered when he continued. "I was rude. I should thank you for spending time with my daughter." He smiled. "Please, stay for supper and let me make it up to you."

Lori glanced away, knowing this man was trouble. She wasn't his type. Men like Jace Yeager didn't give her much notice. *Keep it light.* "We're getting an early start on the Christmas pageant. How are you at playing the part of an angel?"

Cassie giggled.

He smiled, too. "Maybe I'd do better playing a devil."

She had no doubt. "I guess I could write in that part."

She knew coming here would be crossing the line. They worked together, but it needed to stay business. Instead she was in Jace Yeager's home. And even with all the unfinished projects he had going on, it already felt like a real home. It set off a different kind of yearning inside her. That elusive traditional family she'd always wanted. Something all the money from her inheritance couldn't buy her.

Two hours later, Jace finished up the supper dishes, recalling the laughter he heard from his daughter and their guest.

It let him know how much Cassie missed having another female around. A mother. He tensed. Shelly Yeager—soon-to-be Layfield—had never been the typical mother. She'd only cared about money and her social status and her daughter ranked a poor second. More than anything he wanted to give Cassie a home and a life where she'd grow up happy and well-adjusted. He could only do that if she was with him. He'd do whatever it took to keep it that way.

In the past, money, mostly his, had pacified Shelly. Now, she'd landed another prospective husband, a rich one. So she had even more power to keep turning the screws on him, threatening to take Cassie back.

He climbed the steps to his daughter's bedroom and found her already dressed in pajamas. Lori was sitting with her on the canopy bed reading her a story.

His chest tightened at the domestic scene. They looked so much alike they could be mother and daughter. He quickly shook away the thought and walked in.

"The end," Lori said as she closed the book and Cassie yawned.

"I see a very sleepy little girl."

"No, Daddy." She yawned again. "I want another story."

He shook his head and looked at Lori. "The rule is only one bedtime story on a school night." He checked his watch. "Besides, we've taken up enough of Lori's time tonight."

Cassie looked at her. "I'm sorry."

"No, don't be sorry, Cassie." She hugged the girl. "I enjoyed every minute. I told you I read to my nephew."

Cassie's eyes brightened. "Daddy, Lori's nephew, Zack, is coming here to live. He's going to be in my class."

"That'll be nice. How about we talk about it tomorrow? Now, you go to sleep."

Jace watched Lori and his daughter exchange another hug, then she got up and left the room. After he kissed his daughter, he turned off the light and headed downstairs. He found Lori putting on her coat and heading for the back door.

"Trying to make your escape?"

She turned around. "I'm sure you're tired, too."

He walked to her. "I think you might win that contest. Spending four hours with my daughter, not counting the time at school, had to be exhausting."

She smiled. "Remember, I'm a trained professional."

His gut tightened at the teasing glint in her incredible eyes. "And I know my daughter. She can try anyone's patience, but she's the love of my life."

He saw Lori's expression turn a little sad. "She's a lucky little girl." She turned away. "I should get home."

Something made him go after her. Before she could make it to the back door, he reached for her and turned her around. "I wish things could have been different for you, Lori. I'm sorry that you had to suffer as a child."

She shook her head. "It was a long time ago and I've dealt with it."

"Hey, you can't fool a foster kid. I was in the system most of my life. We're experts on rejection."

Her gaze went to his, those brown eyes compelling. "What happened to your family?"

"My parents were in a car accident when I was eight. What relatives I had didn't want me, so I went into foster care."

"Oh, Jace," she whispered.

Her little breathless gasp caused a different kind of reaction from him. Then he saw the tears in her eyes.

His chest tightened. "Hey, don't. I survived. Look at me. A success story."

Jace reached out and touched her cheek. The next thing he knew he pulled her toward him, then wrapped her in his arms. He silenced a groan as he felt her sweet body tucked against his. It had been so long since he'd held a woman. So long since he'd felt the warmth, the glorious softness.

He pulled back trying to put some space between them, but couldn't seem to let her go. His gaze went to her face; her dark eyes mirrored the same desire. He was in big trouble.

He lowered his head and whispered, "This is probably a really bad idea." His mouth brushed over hers, once, then again. Each time she made a little breathy sound that ripped at his gut until he couldn't resist any longer and he captured her tempting mouth.

She wrapped her arms around his neck and leaned into him as her fingers played with the hair at his nape. He pushed his tongue into her mouth and found heaven. She was the sweetest woman he'd ever tasted, and the last thing he ever wanted to do was stop. He wanted so much more, but also knew he couldn't have it.

He tore his mouth away and took a step back. "Damn, woman. You pack a punch. I just can't…"

"It's okay." She pulled her coat tighter. "It would be crazy to start something."

He couldn't believe how badly he wanted to. "Right. Bad idea. We're business partners. Besides, I have room for only one female in my life. Cassie."

Her gaze wouldn't meet his. "I should go."

"Let me walk you out."

"No, you don't need to do that. It's too cold."

He tried to make light of the situation. "Right now, I could use a blast of cold air." He followed her out. Grabbing his coat off the hook, he slipped it on as they went through the mudroom. The frigid air hit him hard as they hurried out to the well-lit driveway and around to her side of the car.

"Nice ride." He glanced over the four-wheel-drive SUV. "You're ready for the snow." He held on to the door so she couldn't rush off. "Are you coming by the site tomorrow?"

"No." She paused. "Unless you need me for something."

He found he wanted to see her again. "I guess not."

"Okay then, good night, Jace."

"Thank you, Lori. Thank you for being there for Cassie."

"You're welcome. Goodbye." She shut her door and started the engine and was backing out of the drive before Jace could stop her. That was the last thing he needed to do. He didn't need to be involved with this woman.

Any woman.

It would be a long time before he could trust again. But if he let her, Lori Hutchinson could come close to melting his cold, cold heart.

Lori had spent the past two days at the bank where she'd been trying to familiarize herself with her father's business dealings. How many people expected her to fail at this?

She'd stayed far away from Jace Yeager, although that didn't change the fact that she'd been thinking about him.

Had he been thinking about her? No. If he had been, wouldn't he have called? Or maybe he'd resisted, knowing getting involved could create more problems.

Lori looked up from the desk as Erin walked into

the office. The receptionist had been such a big help to her, going through files and being the liaison between Lori and Dennis Bradley's office.

Erin sat down in the chair across from the desk. "I found this in an old personnel file, and it's kind of interesting. Kaley Sims did used to work for Mr. Hutchinson. It states that she managed his properties up until two years ago."

Lori had found this woman's notes on several contracts. "Why isn't she working for him now?"

Erin gave her a funny look and glanced away.

"You know something?"

"It's just some bank gossip, but there might have been something between Kaley and Mr. Hutchinson, beyond professional."

So her father had someone after his divorce. "I take it they were discreet."

"They went to business and social functions together, but no one saw any signs of affection between them."

Lori shrugged. "Maybe that's the reason Kaley left here. She wanted more from Lyle."

"If you want to talk to her, I could call her mother and see if she's available to come back to work here."

Lori needed the help. "I guess it wouldn't hurt to call. I sure could use the help, especially someone who already knows the business. I don't want to put in twelve-hour days."

Had Lyle Hutchinson become that much of a recluse that all he did was work? She was curious. Had her father driven off Kaley?

"Okay, I'll make the call tomorrow," Erin said as she stood. "Is there anything more you need today?"

Lori checked her watch. It was after five o'clock. "I'm sorry. You need to get home."

"Normally I'd stay, but I have a date tonight."

Lori smiled, feeling a little twinge of envy, and immediately thought about Jace. Since the kiss she hadn't heard a word from him in two days. *Stop.* She couldn't let one kiss affect her. She wasn't a teenager. "Well, you're great, Erin. I'm grateful to have all your help." She paused. "How would you like to be my assistant?"

"Really?"

"Really. But you have to promise to stay in college. We can schedule hours around your classes, and you'll get a pay raise."

"Oh, wow. Thank you. I'd love to be your assistant." Erin reached out and shook her hand. "And everyone thought you coming to town would be a bad thing."

"Oh, they did, huh?"

This time, Erin hesitated. "I think they thought that a lot of jobs might be lost." The pretty brunette beamed. "Instead, you've come here and come up with ideas so people can save their homes, and you're helping women advance, too."

Lori was happy she could do something. "So it's a good thing?"

"Very good." The girl turned and left the office.

Lori sank back into her father's overstuffed leather chair. "Lyle Hutchinson, you must have really been some kind of tyrant. What made you so unhappy?"

She thought about the sizable amount of money Lyle had acquired over the years. When the waiting period was over next year, she'd never be able to spend it all. She could give the money away. Right now, she received a large income just from his properties.

Sadness hit her hard. Seeing how her father lived, she realized he'd died a lonely man. Outside his few male friends, he didn't go out with anyone. "I was always there, Dad. Just a call away. Your daughter. I would have loved to spend time with you."

It might be too late for a family with her father, but there was a second chance, because she had a sister and nephew. Gina and Zack would always be her family.

A few days had passed and Jace hadn't been able to get Lori, or the kiss, out of his head. Even working nonstop at the site couldn't keep his mind from wandering back to Lori Hutchinson. Until work came to a sudden halt when problems with the staircase came up and didn't meet code. They had to make some changes in the design.

He needed Lori's okay to move ahead with the architect's revisions. He went by the bank, but discovered she was at home. So that was where he was headed when he realized he was looking forward to seeing her. Glad for the excuse.

He pulled up out front, sat there a moment to pull it together. Then he jerked open the door and got out of his truck. The early November day was cold. He looked up at the gray sky, glad that they'd finished the outside of the building. At the very least they would get some rain.

He walked up to the porch, but slowed his steps at the door, feeling his heart rate accelerate.

He hadn't seen Lori since the night at his house. When she had been in his arms. He released a breath. Even time away didn't change the fact that he was eager to see her.

Maggie opened the door with her usual smile. "Mr. Yeager. It's nice to see you again."

He stepped inside. "Hi, Maggie. Is Lori here?" He held up his folder. "I have more papers for her to sign," he said, suddenly hearing the noises coming from upstairs.

"Oh, she's here." Maggie grinned. "Been working all day trying to get things finished before her sister and nephew's arrival tomorrow. Charlie's helping." There was a big thud and Maggie looked concerned. "But maybe you should have a look."

Jace nodded. He headed for the stairs and took them two at a time to shorten the trip. He walked down the hall and was surprised when he found the source of the noise. It was coming from the room across from Lori's childhood bedroom.

He looked in the slightly open door and found Charlie and Lori kneeling on the floor with sections of wood spread out. The two were engrossed in reading a sheet of directions.

Lori brushed back a strand of hair, revealing her pretty face. Then his heart went soaring and his body heated up as she reached for something and her jeans pulled taut over her cute, rounded bottom.

"It says right here that *A* goes into *B*. Okay we got that, but I can't find the next piece." She held up the sheet of paper. "Do you see this one?"

Hiding his amusement, Jace stepped into the room. "Could you two use some help?"

They both swung around. "Mr. Yeager," Charlie said and got to his feet. "Oh, yes, we could use your expertise. And since you're here to help, I'll go do my work." The older man left, looking relieved.

Jace turned back at Lori. "What are you building?"

"Bunk beds," she offered.

Jace pulled off his jacket as he glanced over the stacks of boxes. "Why not buy it assembled?"

Lori stood. "I didn't have time to go to Durango, so I got them online. I didn't realize it would come in boxes."

"You should have called me. I would have sent Mac over." He took the paper from her. Their hands brushed, and he quickly busied himself by looking over the directions. "Okay, let's lay out the rails and the end pieces."

Lori took one end and he took the other. He set the bolts, then went to her end. He was close and could breathe in her scent, which distracted the hell out of him. He finally got the bolt tightened. He got up and went to the other side, away from temptation, but she followed him.

Over the next hour, they'd become engrossed in building the elaborate bunk-bed set. They stood back and looked over their accomplishment.

"Not bad work." He glanced at the woman beside him and saw her blink. "What's wrong?"

She shook her head. "Zack is going to love it. He's had to share a room with his mother the past few months. Thank you for this."

"Not a problem," he told her. "You helped me out with Cassie. I know how much you want to make a home for your sister and your nephew."

"They've had a rough time of it lately." She put on a smile. "It's going to be great for them to be here."

Jace looked around the freshly painted blue room. "I thought you were going to put Zack in your old bedroom."

She shrugged. "I tried, but I couldn't bring myself

to touch it." She looked at him and he saw the pain in her eyes. "I guess I'm still trying to figure out why my father kept it the same all these years. Crazy, huh?"

Unable to help himself, he draped his arm across her shoulders. "It's okay, Lori. You have a lot to work through. You've pulled up your roots and come back here. There's a lot to deal with."

She looked up. "But I have the funds now to take care of my family."

That was the one thing that kind of bothered him. He'd been pretty well-off financially before his divorce, but to have a woman with so much money when he was trying to scrape by hit him in his pride. But he truly thought it bothered her more.

"So how does it feel to have that kind of money?"

She scrunched up her nose. "Oddly strange," she admitted. "It's far too much. I'm the kind of girl who's had to work all my life, and when I lost my job a few months ago, I was really worried about what was going to happen, especially for Gina and Zack."

"They have you now."

She looked up at him, her eyes bright and rich in color. "And I have them. I wouldn't stay here in Destiny, money or no money, if they couldn't be with me. Their safety and well-being is the most important thing to me."

He frowned. "Why wouldn't they be safe here?"

She glanced away. "It's just a worry I have."

He touched her chin to get her to look at him. "Lori, what aren't you telling me? Is someone threatening you or your family?"

She finally looked at him. "It's Gina's ex-husband. He'll be getting out of jail soon."

"Why did he go to jail?"

"Look, Jace, I'm not sure Gina wants anyone to know her private business."

"I'm not a gossip. If your family needs protection then I want to help."

Lori was surprised at his offer. She wasn't used to anyone helping them. "Eric is in for drug possession and spousal abuse. He swore when he got out he'd make Gina pay for having him arrested."

She felt Jace tense. "So that's why you were headed out of state?"

She nodded.

"Does this Eric guy know where Gina is moving to?"

"No one knows. We haven't even told Zack. I want so badly for Gina to make a life here. She has full custody of her son, but we're still afraid of what the man might do."

"This house has a security system. I hope you're using it."

She nodded.

"And I think you should have protection for yourself, also. You're worth a lot of money and you could be a target for threats from this guy. Maybe a security guard isn't out of the question."

"I can't let my life be dictated by a coward."

Jace clenched his fists. "I don't care for a creep who gets his jollies by beating women, either, but you still need to take precautions. Not an armed guard, but maybe a security man disguised as a gardener or handyman."

She hesitated. "If Gina will agree."

"What about you? I'm sure you've had some run-ins with your brother-in-law."

Lori shivered, recalling Eric's threats.

Jace's eyes narrowed. "Did he hurt you, too?"

"Just a few shoves here and there, but I couldn't let him hurt Gina."

He cursed and walked away, then came back to her. He reached out and cupped her face. "He put his hands on you, Lori. No man ever has the right to do that unless the woman wants it."

She stared into his eyes. That was the problem. She wanted Jace's hands on her. Badly.

CHAPTER SEVEN

JACE had trouble letting go of Lori. He knew the minute he touched her again this would happen.

He cursed under his breath. "This isn't a good idea." His gaze searched her pretty face, those bedroom eyes, then he stopped at her perfect rosy mouth. He suddenly felt like a man dying of thirst. Especially when her tongue darted out over her lips. With a groan, he leaned down and brushed his mouth across hers, hearing her quick intake of breath.

"I swore I'd stay away from you. We shouldn't start something…." His mouth brushed over hers again and then again. "My life doesn't need to get any more complicated."

"Mine, either," she whispered.

He fought the smile, but it didn't stop the hunger, or the anticipation of the kiss he so desperately wanted more than his next breath.

Then Lori took the decision out of his hands as she rose up on her toes and pressed her mouth against his. That was all it took. His arms circled her waist and he pulled her against him, unable to tolerate the space between them any longer. Their bodies meshed so easily it was as if they were meant to be together. All he knew was he didn't want to let her go anytime soon.

His mouth slanted over hers, wanting to taste her, but all too quickly they were getting carried away.

He tore his mouth from hers, and trailed kisses along her jaw to her ear. "I could get drunk on you." Then he let his tongue trace her earlobe, feeling her shiver. He found her mouth again for another hungry kiss.

Then suddenly the sound of his cell phone brought him back to reality. He stepped back, and his gaze was drawn to Lori's thoroughly kissed mouth. Desire shot through him and he had to turn away.

"Yeager," he growled into the phone.

"Hey, Jace," Toby said. "What happened? I thought you were coming right back."

He glanced over his shoulder at Lori. "Sorry, something came up. I'm heading back now." He shut his phone. "I'm needed at the site."

"Of course," Lori said, wrapping honey-blond strands behind her ear. "I can't thank you enough for your help. I couldn't have done this on my own."

Unable to resist, he went back to her and stole another kiss. They were both breathless by the time he released her. "Your sister and nephew arrive tomorrow, right?"

She nodded.

"Okay, I'll have a security guy in place here before you get back from the airport." When Lori started to disagree, he put his finger over those very inviting lips. "He'll work with Charlie so Gina doesn't have to know. I want you and your family safe."

Lori smiled. "I wasn't going to disagree. I think it's a good idea."

He blinked. "You're agreeing with me? That's a first."

"Don't get used to it, Yeager."

The next afternoon, Lori had agreed to let Charlie drive her father's town car the 47 miles to the Durango airport to pick up Gina and Zack.

She couldn't hide her excitement as she watched her sister and nephew come out of the terminal. She gave them a big hug, then herded them into the backseat of the car while Charlie stowed the few belongings in the trunk.

They talked all the way to Destiny. It was as if they'd been apart for months instead of only two weeks.

Lori kept hugging her seven-year-old nephew beside her in the backseat. She'd missed him. "Zack. I was able to work in the second grade classroom last week and met your teacher, Mrs. Miller. I think you're going to like her."

The little dark-haired child didn't look happy. "But I don't know any kids."

"The class knows you're coming. And there's Ellie and Cassie, who will help you learn your way around the school."

"Girls?"

That brought a smile as Lori looked at her sister. Although beautiful, with her rich, dark brown hair and wide green eyes, Regina Williams Lowell looked a little pale and far too thin. Lori hoped she could erase her sister's fear once she knew she was safe living in Destiny. And her son would blossom here, too.

"It might take a little time, Zack, but I know you'll make lots of friends."

They drove through town, past the square and fountain, then down the row of storefronts. "Just wait. Soon they'll be putting up a big Christmas tree with colorful lights. The whole town will be decorated."

"Can we have a Christmas tree at your house?"

Suddenly Lori got excited. This was going to be a special holiday. And a new year that meant a fresh beginning for all of them. "You bet we can. And you can pick out a really big one."

Zack grinned as they pulled through the gate. "Wow!" The boy's eyes lit up. "Mom, are we really going to live here?"

"We sure are." Gina looked like a kid herself. "Although, I can hardly believe it myself."

Lori glanced at her sister's face. "That was my first reaction, too. Welcome to Hutchinson House."

Charlie drove up the long drive and stopped in front of the house. He opened the back door and helped them out, then sent them up the porch steps.

Maggie swung open the front door and opened her arms. "Welcome, welcome," the older woman said as she swept them inside the warm house. First, the older woman embraced Zack, then Gina.

"We're so happy you're here. Oh, my, and to have a child in this big house again is wonderful."

"It's so big," Zack said. "What if I get lost?"

"Don't worry. Charlie will show you around. The important thing to remember is there are two sets of stairs. One leads down here." Maggie pointed to the circular staircase. "Most important, the other one leads to the kitchen and I'm usually there."

Zack looked a little more comfortable after the quick explanation.

Maggie turned to Gina and smiled. "Goodness, my, you look so much like Lorelei and your mother. Your coloring might be different, but there's no doubt you're sisters. And both beautiful."

Her sister seemed embarrassed. "Thank you."

"How was your flight?"

"Not too bad, especially sitting in first class." Gina glanced at Lori. "It was a big treat for Zack and me."

"Well, we're planning on a lot of treats for Master Zack." The older woman placed her hands on the boy's shoulders. "After you go and see your new bedroom, come down to the kitchen so you can tell me all your favorite foods. And if it's okay with your mother you can sample some of my cookies." Maggie raised a hand and glanced at Gina. "I promise not to spoil his appetite for our special dinner tonight."

"The way my son eats, I doubt anything can." Gina smiled, which made Lori hopeful that her sister would start relaxing.

"We're also having a couple of guests for dinner," Maggie announced. "Mr. Yeager and his daughter, Cassie. And before you frown, Zack, the girl has a horse. That's a good friend to have."

Lori was surprised by the news, and a little too happy, feeling a stir of excitement. Maybe he was bringing the security guard they'd talked about.

Maggie gave her the answer. "Jace has something to discuss with you. So I invited them both to dinner."

Her nephew called to her. "Can I go see my new bedroom, Aunt Lori?"

"Sure. How about we all head up and see it?"

The child ran ahead of them, following Charlie up the steps with the bags.

Lori hung back with Gina. "Lori, you never said the place was a—" she looked around the huge entry, her eyes wide "—mansion."

"Okay, so the Hutchinson family liked things on the large size. Now that you and Zack are here, it's already starting to feel more like a home." She hugged her sister again. "I want you and Zack to think of this place as home. More important, I want you to feel safe here."

Gina looked a little panicked. "Just so long as Eric never finds us."

Another precaution had been for Gina to take back her maiden name, Williams.

"If he shows up in Destiny, you can believe he'll be arrested." Jace had convinced her to let Sheriff Reed Larkin in on the situation.

"Does everyone in town know?"

Lori shook her head. "No, only the people who work here at the house. And Jace Yeager, my business partner. He suggested that I hire some security." Lori raised a hand. "Only just as a precaution."

"That has to cost a lot of money."

Lori smiled. "Look at this place, Gina. Lyle Hutchinson might have been a lousy father, but he knew how to make money. And taking care of you and Zack is worth whatever it costs."

Tears filled her sister's eyes. "Thank you."

Before Lori started crying, too, she said, "Come on, I hope you like your bedroom. It's got a connecting bath with Zack's room."

They started up the steps arm in arm. "I can't imagine I wouldn't love it."

"If you don't like it, you can redo it. You're the one

with experience. In fact, I'd be happy if you would redo the entire place."

Gina turned to Lori. "Decorating a boutique window doesn't make me a professional." She looked around. "It's so grand as it is."

Lori knew what her sister had been thinking. There had been a lot of times when their living quarters hadn't been that great, especially when Gina was married. Being a school dropout, Eric hadn't been able to do much, and he spent his paycheck on alcohol instead of diapers.

"This is our fresh start, Gina. You don't have to worry about Eric anymore. I'm not going to let anything happen to either you or Zack."

Lori prayed that was a promise she could keep.

Three hours later, Jace walked up the steps to the Hutchinson home, carrying a bottle of wine and flowers. He normally didn't take Cassie out on a school night, but this was a special occasion and he knew how it was to be the new kid in town.

Okay, the truth was he wanted to see Lori. He'd tried to keep focused on work, but she was messing with his head. Last night he couldn't sleep, recalling their kisses, but he knew from now on that he had to keep his hands to himself. If Shelly got wind of any of this, she would make his life miserable just for the hell of it.

He had to focus on Cassie and getting the project completed on time. That was all. Once he had custody settled, he could think about a life for himself.

The front door opened and a little boy stuck his head out. "Hi," he said shyly.

His daughter answered back. "Hi. You're Zack. I'm Cassie Yeager. You're going to be in my class at school."

The boy looked up at Jace as if asking for help. His daughter never had a problem with being shy.

"I'm Jace. I think your aunt is expecting us."

Zack nodded. "You want to come in?"

"Sounds good. It's a little cold out here."

The door opened wider as another woman appeared. She smiled, showing off the resemblance to Lori.

"Hello, you must be Gina. I'm Jace Yeager. I'm Lori's business partner."

She took his hand. "It's nice to meet you."

"This is my daughter, Cassie."

His daughter beamed as she came up to Gina. "Hi, Miss Gina. My dad brought you flowers and for Miss Lori, wine. And I bought Zack a school sweatshirt." She held up the burgundy-colored shirt with Destiny Elementary School printed on it.

"Hello, Cassie. That's very nice."

Cassie turned to Zack. "My dad said you have a new bedroom."

"Yeah, it's cool."

"Can I see it?"

Zack looked at his mother for permission. With Gina's nod the two seven-year-olds took off upstairs.

"My son's a little shy," Gina admitted.

"Well, that won't last long if Cassie has anything to say about it."

He finally got a smile out of the pretty dark-haired woman with green eyes. There was definitely a strong resemblance between the two sisters, except for their coloring. Both women were lovely.

"Here, these are for you. Welcome to Destiny."

He watched her blush as she took the bouquet. "Thank you."

"It's rough having to pick up and move everything. I had to do it about six months ago, but it was worth it. Destiny is a wonderful place to raise kids. Cassie loves it here."

"I'm glad." Gina hesitated. "Lori said she told you about my…situation."

He watched her hesitation, maybe more embarrassment. "I assure you, Gina, no one else will know about your past. It's no one's business. Your sister only wants you safe. I agreed to help her take some precautions."

"I appreciate it, really. I'm sure Eric wouldn't think to look for us here. He knows nothing about Lori's father." She sighed. "But I wouldn't put anything past him. So I thank you for the extra security."

Jace was about to speak when Lori came down the steps. She was wearing a black turtleneck sweater and gray slacks. He was caught up in her grace as she descended the winding stairs. She smiled at him, and his insides went all haywire.

Lori felt Jace's gaze on her and it made her nervous, also a little warm. She'd missed seeing him. The last time had only been a little over twenty-four hours ago when he'd helped her with the bed, and they almost fell into it. A warm shiver moved up her spine. How did he feel about it?

She walked across the tiled floor, seeing her sister holding flowers. That was so nice of him. "Hi, Jace."

"Lori."

She went to him. "Sorry, I wasn't here when you arrived. I just saw Cassie upstairs."

"Has she reorganized Zack's bedroom yet?"

Lori couldn't help but laugh. "I think he's safe for the moment."

Gina spoke up. "Excuse me. I'll go put these in water, then go up and have the kids wash up for dinner." She turned and walked to the kitchen.

Jace looked at Lori. "I don't want to barge in on your family dinner."

"You're not at all. You're always welcome here," she told him, knowing that was probably admitting too much. "Maggie loves to have company. She hasn't been able to cook this much in a long time."

"Anytime she wants company tell her I'll be here." He held up the bottle. "I brought wine."

Lori smiled. "Why don't we open it?"

"Lead the way," he said and they started toward the dining room. Lori watched as he stared at the dark burgundy wallpaper, dark-stained wainscoting and long, long table with the upholstered chairs, also dark.

"It's pretty bad. This room is like a mausoleum. It's going to be my first redecorating project. In fact, I'll put Gina in charge. I hope you don't mind eating in the kitchen."

"I prefer the kitchen." He glanced down at his jeans and sweater pulled over a collared shirt. He followed Lori to the sideboard. In actuality, he preferred her over it all, but he tried to stay focused on the conversation. "As you can see, I'm not dressed for anything fancy."

Lori thought he was dressed perfectly. The man would look good in...nothing. Oh, no. *Don't think about that.* She busied herself by opening a drawer and searching for a corkscrew. Once she found it, she handed it to him, then crossed to the glass-front hutch and took out two crystal wineglasses.

"Gina won't drink, so we'll have to toast my sister and nephew's arrival on our own."

"I think I can handle that." He managed to uncork the bottle and when she brought over the glasses, he filled them with the rosy liquid.

He held out the stemmed glass to her. She brushed his hand and tried to remain calm. It was only a drink, she told herself.

Jace picked up his. "To yours, Gina's and Zack's new home," he said.

Lori took a slow sip, allowing herself to enjoy the sweet taste. She took another, and soon the alcohol went to her head, making her feel a little more relaxed. Then her eyes connected with Jace, and suddenly her heart was racing once again.

"This tastes nice," she said, unable to get her mouth to work. "I mean, I'm not much of a drinker, but I like this."

His deep sapphire gaze never left hers as he set his glass down on the sideboard. "Let me see." Then he leaned forward and touched his mouth to hers.

She froze, unable to do anything but feel as his firm mouth caressed her lips, coaxing her to open for him with a stroke of his tongue.

She whimpered as her hand rested against his chest, feeling his pounding heart. She only ached for more.

He pulled back a little. "You're right. Sweet." He took her glass from her and set it down beside his. "But I need another taste to be sure."

He bent down and took her mouth again. She went willingly as her arms circled his neck, and she wanted to close out the rest of the world. Just the two of them. She refused to think about how stupid it was to let this happen with Jace. When his tongue stroked against hers, and he drew her against his body, she lost all common sense.

Then it quickly returned when the sound of footsteps overhead alerted them to the fact that the kids were coming.

He broke off, and pressed his head against hers. "Damn, Lorelei Hutchinson, if you don't make me forget my own name."

She could only manage a nod. Then he leaned forward again. "Not that you don't look beautiful thoroughly kissed, but you might have to answer too many questions."

She smoothed her hair. "Tell everyone I'll be in shortly." She took off, knowing she was a fool when it came to this man. It had to stop before someone got hurt.

Jace had trouble concentrating on his pot roast dinner. Why couldn't he keep his hands off Lori? She wasn't even his type. Not that he had a type. He'd sworn off women for the time being. So why had he been trying to play tonsil hockey with her just thirty minutes ago?

"Daddy?"

He turned to his daughter. "What, Cassie?"

"Can Zack go riding with me tomorrow?"

Jace glanced at Gina and saw her concerned look. "Maybe it's a little cold right now, sweetheart. Let Zack and his mother get settled in first. Besides, you both have school all day."

Those pretty blue eyes blinked up at him. "I know, Daddy," she said. "I'm gonna help Zack get used to the class."

Jace fought a smile and stole a glance at Lori, then at the poor boy who'd become his daughter's newest project. "I'm sure Zack appreciates all your help, sweetheart, but remember, Miss Lori is a teacher. She can help, too."

The child looked deflated. "Oh."

"I can sure use your help," Lori said. "And we're all going to be working on the Christmas play together. I'm sure Zack would like to do that."

"I guess," he said. "Are there other boys in the play?"

Cassie nodded. "Everyone is in the play. Cody Peters and Owen Hansen and Willie Burns." She smiled. "And now, you."

Jace wasn't sure he liked how his daughter was smiling at Zack. *Oh, no, not her first crush.*

Maggie came in with dessert and after everyone enjoyed the chocolate cake, the kids were excused and went up to Zack's bedroom.

"Seems like they've become fast friends," Gina said. "I thank you, Jace. Your daughter is helping my son a lot." She glanced at her sister. "I hated that Zack had to go through all the pain of the last few years."

"You need to put that in the past. This is a new start."

Lori reached over and covered her sister's hand. "It's a new beginning, Gina. We're going to keep you safe."

"Lori's right," Jace told her. "The security guard is on duty as we speak. Wyatt McCray will be touring the grounds during the night. He's moved into the room behind the garage. His cover will be he's working with Charlie. No one is going to hurt you or your son again."

Tears formed in Gina's eyes. "Thank you."

Lori spoke up. "Has Eric been released yet?"

"Detective Rogers said he is scheduled to get out this Friday."

"Good." Jace nodded. "You and Zack were gone before he had a chance to know what your plans were. The fewer people who know the better. So we three, Maggie, Charlie, Wyatt and Sheriff Larkin are the only people who know about your situation. You're divorced, and your past life is private."

"I'm grateful, Jace. Thank you." Gina stood. "I think I'll go check on the kids."

Lori watched her sister leave. "She's still scared to death."

"I know," Jace said, hating that he couldn't do more. "And I almost wish the creep would show up here so I could get my hands on him."

"No, I don't want that man anywhere near them ever again. Zack still has nightmares." She put on a smile. "Thank you for all your help."

His gaze held hers for longer than necessary. "Hey, we're partners."

Problem was, he wanted to be so much more.

CHAPTER EIGHT

By the end of the week Gina and Zack had settled in and were getting into a routine. Her nephew had started school and was making new friends. Of course, Cassie was still taking charge of Zack's social schedule.

Life was great, Lori thought, as she arrived at the bank that cold, gray November morning. Thank goodness her car had seat warmers to ward off the near-freezing temperatures. She thought about the upcoming holidays and couldn't help but smile. Her family would all be together.

She also thought of Jace. She wanted to invite him and Cassie to Thanksgiving at the house. Would he come? The memory of the kisses they'd shared caused a shiver down her spine. She was crazy to think about a future with the man, especially when he'd been telling her all along he didn't want to get involved.

As she entered her office, she decided not to go to the construction site unless absolutely necessary. Besides, she had plenty to do at the bank to keep her busy for a long time. She looked down at the several stacks of files and paperwork covering the desktop. The last thing she wanted to do was spend all her time managing the number of properties, and the rest of the time at the bank. If only she could hire someone to oversee it all. And she didn't trust the "three amigos" loan officers to handle things on their own. They'd already thought she was in over her head. Maybe she was, but she wasn't going to let them see it.

She'd been working nearly two hours when there was a knock on the door. "Come in," Lori called.

Erin walked in. She wore a simple black A-line skirt and a pin-striped red-and-white blouse. She was carrying a coffee mug and a white paper sack. "Break time?"

"Thank you, I could use it. Everything is getting a little blurry."

"You should have more than coffee. Helen sent over some scones from the Silver Spoon. A thank-you for putting a six-month moratorium on foreclosures."

Lori thought of her own childhood after her mother remarried. They'd had some rough times over the years. "I refuse to let this bank play Scrooge especially with Christmas coming soon. The first thing on the agenda for the first of next year is reworking these loans."

Erin smiled. "You know, the other bank officers aren't happy with your decision."

Lori took a sip of her drink. "Yes. Mr. Neal has already decided to retire." She thought about the generous retirement package her father had given him. He wouldn't be giving up his lifestyle.

"Oh, I almost forgot," Erin said. "I located Kaley Sims. She's working for a management company in Durango. I have the phone number."

"Good. Would you put in a call to her and see if she's willing to talk with me?"

"Of course. Anything else?"

Erin was so efficient at her job, Lori wasn't sure what she would have done without her.

"There is one thing. In looking over my father's properties, I found a place called—" she searched through the list "—Hidden Hills Lodge. I'm not sure if it's a rental property, or what. It doesn't show any reported income."

"Maybe it was a place Mr. Hutchinson had for his personal use. Do you want me to find out more about it?"

Lori shook her head. "No, you have more than enough to do now." Maybe she would look into this herself. She had a great GPS in her new car. Surely she could find her way. She stood. "I'm going to be gone the rest of the afternoon. If you need me, call me on my cell phone."

Maybe it was time she delved a little further into her father's past and the opportunity was right in front of her.

Later that afternoon, Jace got out of his truck as snow flurries floated in the air, clinging to his coat and hat. He took a breath as he walked to the bank. Okay, he'd been avoiding going anywhere he might see Lori Hutchinson. He couldn't seem to keep his hands off the woman, but since he needed her signature on some changes in the project, he didn't have a choice.

He walked through the doors and Erin greeted him. "Is Miss Hutchinson in?"

"No, she's not. She left about noon."

"She go home?"

"No, I've tried to reach her there. I also tried her cell

phone, but it goes to voice mail." Erin frowned. "I'm worried about her, especially with this weather."

Suddenly Jace was concerned, too. "And she didn't say where she was going? A property? Out to the site?"

"That's what I'm worried about. I think she might have gone to the Hidden Hills Lodge."

"Where is this place?"

Erin sat down at her desk and printed out directions from the computer. Jace looked them over. He wasn't sure about this area, only that it was pretty rural.

He wrote down his number and handed it to Erin. "Give me a call if Lori gets in touch with you."

He left as he pulled out his cell phone and gave Claire Keenan a call, asking if she'd watch Cassie a little later, then he hung up and glanced up at the sky. An odd feeling came over him, and not a good one. "Where are you, Lori?"

An hour later, Lori had turned off the highway to a private road, just as her GPS had instructed her to do. She shifted her car into four-wheel drive and began to move slowly along the narrowing path.

It wasn't long before she realized coming today wasn't a good idea. Deciding to go back, she shifted her SUV into Reverse and pushed on the gas pedal, and all that happened was the tires began to spin.

"Great. Please, I don't need this." She glanced out her windshield as her wipers pushed away the blowing snow, which didn't look like it was going to stop anytime soon.

She took out her cell phone. No signal. The one thing that was working was her GPS and it showed her destination was a quarter mile up the road. What should she do? Stay in the car, or walk to Hidden Hills Lodge?

She buttoned her coat, wrapped her scarf around her neck and grabbed a flashlight. She turned on her emergency blinkers and climbed out as the blowing snow hit her. She started her trek up the dirt road and her fear rose. What if she got lost and froze to death? Her thoughts turned to Gina and Zack. And Jace. She cared more about the man than she even wanted to admit. And she wanted to see him again. She quickened her pace, keeping to the center of the dirt road.

Ten minutes later, cold and tired, she finally saw the structure through the blowing snow. It was almost like a mirage in the middle of the trees. She hurried up the steps to the porch and tried the door. Locked.

"Key, where are you?" she murmured, hating to break a window. It took a few minutes, but she found a metal box behind the log bench. After unlocking the dead bolt with nearly frozen fingers, she hurried into the dark structure and closed the door. She reached for the switch on the wall and light illuminated the huge main room. With a gasp, she glanced around. The walls were made out of rough logs and the open-beam ceiling showed off the loft area overhead. Below the upstairs were two doorways leading to bedrooms. The floors were high-gloss pine with large area rugs and overstuffed furniture was arranged in front of a massive fireplace. She found a thermostat on the wall and flipped it, immediately hearing the heater come on.

Shivering, Lori walked to the fireplace and added some logs. With the aid of the gas starter, flames shot over the wood. She sat on the hearth, feeling warmth begin to seep through her chilled body.

Once warmed, she got up and looked around. The kitchen was tucked in the back side of the structure, revealing granite counters and dark cabinets.

She checked out the two bedrooms and a bath on the main floor. Then she climbed up to the loft and found another bedroom. One of the walls was all windows with a view of the forest. She walked into the connecting bathroom. This one had a soaker tub and a huge walk-in shower.

"I guess if you have to be stranded in a snowstorm, a mountain retreat isn't a bad place to be." At least she'd stay warm until someone found her. When? Next spring?

She came back downstairs trying to think of a plan to get her back to town, when a sudden noise drew her attention. She froze as the door opened and Jace Yeager walked in.

"Jace!" she cried and leaped into his arms.

He held her close and whispered, "I take it you're happy to see me."

Jace didn't want to let Lori go. Thank God, she was safe. When he found her deserted car, he wasn't sure if she would find cover.

He pulled back. "Are you crazy, woman? Why did you go out in this weather?"

She blinked back the obvious tears in her eyes. "It wasn't this bad when I started out. Besides, I didn't think it was that far. I tried to go back when the weather turned, but my car got stuck. How did you know where I went?"

"I stopped by the bank. Erin was worried because she couldn't get ahold of you."

"No cell service."

Jace pulled out his phone and examined it. "I have a few bars." He walked toward the front door, where the signal seemed to be a little stronger. "I'll call the Keenans." He punched in the number and prayed he could get a message out. Tim answered.

"Tim. It's Jace." He went on to explain what had happened and that Lori was with him. Most importantly they were safe. He asked Tim to keep Cassie, then to call Lori's sister and let her know they wouldn't be back tonight. "Tell Cassie I love her and not to worry."

He flipped the phone closed and looked around the large room, then he turned back to Lori. "Tim will call Gina and let her know you're okay."

Lori's eyes widened. "We're not going back now?"

He shook his head. "Can't risk it. The storm is too bad so we're safer staying put." That was only partly true. He glanced around, knowing being alone with Lori wasn't safe anywhere. "I'd say this isn't a bad place to be stranded in." He looked at her. "This is one of your properties?"

She nodded. "I think my father came here…to get away."

Jace grinned. "So this was Lyle's secret hideaway?"

Lori frowned. "Please, I don't want that picture in my mind."

Jace looked around at the structure. "Well, whatever he used it for, it's well built. And it seems to have all the modern conveniences."

He went on a search, and found two bedrooms, then a utility room off the kitchen. There was a large generator and tankless water system. "Bingo," he called to Lori. "All the conveniences of home. In fact, it's better than back home." He nodded to the fire. "Propane gas for the kitchen stove and most importantly there's heat."

Lori looked at him. "You really think my father used this place for his own personal use?"

Jace shrugged. "Or he let clients use it. Come on, Lori, did you think your father lived like a monk?"

She shrugged. "Truthfully, I hadn't thought much about my father's personal business in a long time. So what if he came here." She walked to the kitchen. "Maybe we should look for something to eat." Opening the cabinets, she found some canned goods, soup, beans and tuna.

Jace opened the refrigerator. Empty, but the freezer was filled with different cuts of meat, steaks, chicken. "I'll say one thing about Lyle. He believed in being pre-pared." He pulled out two steaks. "Hungry?"

She arched an eyebrow. "Are you cooking?"

"Hey, I can cook." He took the meat from the pack-age, put it on a plate and into the microwave to defrost. "I've been on my own for a long time."

Lori had wondered about his childhood since he'd mentioned that he'd been in foster care. "How old were you?"

"At eighteen they release you. So you're on your own," he told her as he found a can of green beans in another cabinet. "I got a job working construction and signed up for college classes."

Jace didn't have it much better than she did, Lori thought. "That had to be hard for you."

"Not too bad," Jace said. "I found out later, I had a small inheritance from my parents. It was in trust until I turned twenty-five." He turned on the broiler in the oven then washed his hands. "I used it to start my company. Yeager Construction."

Lori found she liked listening to Jace talk. He was a confident man, in his words and movements. Okay, so she more than liked him.

The microwave dinged and he took out the meat. "How about a little seasoning for your steak?" He held up a small jar.

"Sure."

He added the rub to the meat. She watched as he worked efficiently to prepare the meal. She couldn't help but wonder about how those broad hands and tapered fingers would feel against her skin.

She suddenly heard her name and looked at him. "What?"

He gave her an odd look. "How do you like your steak?"

"Any way you fix it is fine," she said, not really caring at all. Then he smiled and she couldn't find enough air to draw into her lungs.

He winked. "Medium rare it is," he said and slid the tray into the broiler.

Pull it together, girl, she told herself then went to the cupboard. She got out two plates and some flatware from the drawer, then set the table by the fire. No need for candles. She glanced around the room. It looked so intimate.

She went and found a can of pineapple and opened it, then heated the green beans just as the steaks came off the broiler.

Jace added another log to the fire, then they sat down to dinner. "Man, this looks good. Too bad we can't do a salad and some garlic bread."

"I find it amazing that there's so much food here."

"Your father struck me as well prepared. Hold on a minute." He got up, went into the utility room and came out with a bottle of wine. "In every way."

He opened the bottle and poured two glasses. He took them to the table, sat in his chair and began to cut his steak. "If he used this place, he wanted all the comforts money could buy," Jace said, nodding to the wine.

"I'm wondering who he shared all this with."

Jace took a drink. "You might never know. One thing for sure, Lyle had good taste."

She took a sip from her glass, too, and had to agree. Then she began to eat, discovering she was hungry. "I guess I'm still the daughter who wonders why he was such a loner, not even finding time for his only child."

"We can spend hours on that subject." Jace continued to eat. "Some people aren't cut out for the job of parenting."

She hated that her father's rejection still bothered her after all these years. She wanted to think she'd moved on. Maybe not.

She turned her attention back to the conversation. "Shelly hated anything to do with being a mother," Jace said. "That's why I can't let her have Cassie."

"Does Cassie want to live with her mother?"

"Cassie wants to be *loved* by her mother, but my ex is too selfish. She's been jealous of her daughter since her birth. And I'll do anything to prevent Cassie from taking a backseat to that. I know how it feels."

"Cassie's lucky she has you."

He smiled. "It's easy to love that little girl. I know I spoil her, but she's been so happy since she moved here. I have to make it permanent."

Lori put on a smile. "You're a good father, Jace Yeager." She placed her hand on his arm. "I'll help you in any way I can."

He stopped eating. "What do you mean? Help. I can afford to handle this custody battle on my own."

She shook her head. "I know that. I only meant that I know what it's like to not have a father in my life. I was offering moral support, nothing else. But don't be too bullheaded to take any and everything you can to keep your daughter. She needs you in her life, more than you know." Lori stood and carried her plate to the sink. Her appetite was gone.

He came to her. "I'm sorry, Lori."

She could feel his heat behind her. Good Lord, the man made his presence known. She wanted desperately to lean back into him. "For years Lyle Hutchinson never even acknowledged that I existed. I can't tell you how much that hurt."

She hated feeling needy. When Jace turned her around and touched her cheek, she couldn't deny she wanted his comfort.

"I can't imagine doing that to my child. I don't want to think about Cassie not being in my life. I know from experience that adults do dumb things, and in the end it's the kids that get hurt the most."

Lori felt a tear drop and he wiped it away. "It's not fair."

Jace leaned forward. "I wish I could change it." He brushed his mouth across hers. "I wish I could make you feel better."

She released a shaky breath. "What you're doing is nice."

His blue-eyed gaze searched her face. "Damn, Lori.

What I'm thinking about doing with you isn't nice."
Then he pulled her close and captured her mouth. Desire
burst within her, if possible more intense than ever before, pooling deep in her center. She could feel his heat
even through their clothes as she arched into his body.
She whimpered her need as his tongue danced against
hers.

"You make me want so many things," he breathed
as his tongue tormented her skin. He found his way to
her collarbone. "I want you, Lorelei Hutchinson." His
mouth closed over hers once again, giving her a hint of
the pleasure this man offered her.

She arched against him, her fingers threading
through his hair, holding him close. Mouths slanted,
their tongues mated as his hands moved over her back
and down to her bottom, pulling her closer to feel his
desire.

Jace was on the edge. On hearing her soft moan, he
drew back with his last ounce of sanity. Then he made
the mistake of looking into her eyes and all good inten-
tions flew out the window. "Tell me to stop now, Lori."

She swallowed. "I can't, Jace. I don't want you to
stop."

His heart skipped a beat as he swung her up into his
arms. With a quick glance around, he headed to one of
the rooms under the loft, only caring there was a bed
past the door.

The daylight was fading, but there was enough light
from the main room. He set her down next to a four-
poster bed. He captured her mouth in a long kiss, then
reached behind her and threw back the thick comforter.

He returned to her. "I've dreamed of being with you

like this." He drew her into his arms. "So be sure you want the same."

She nodded.

He let out a frustrated breath. "You have to do better than that, Lori."

"I'm very sure, Jace."

Those big brown eyes looked up at him. He inhaled her soft scent and was lost, so lost that he couldn't think about anything except sharing this intimacy with this special woman.

His mouth descended to hers and the rest of the snowstorm and the world disappeared. There was only the two of them caught up in their own storm.

CHAPTER NINE

SOMETIME around dawn, Jace woke suddenly, aware he wasn't alone in bed. And it wasn't his bed. He blinked and raised his head from the pillow to find Lori beside him. He bit back a groan as images of last night came flooding into his mind.

He'd come looking for her, afraid she'd been stranded in the freak storm. He found her all right, and had given in to temptation. They'd made love last night. Right now her sweet body pressed against his had him aching again.

He lay his head back on the pillow. Why did she have to come into his life now? He didn't have anything to offer her. Not a future anyway. He couldn't let anyone distract him from getting custody of Cassie.

Lori stirred, then rolled over and peered at him through the dim light. Her soft yellow hair was mussed, but definitely added to her sex appeal.

"Hi," she said in a husky voice that had him thinking about forgetting everything and getting lost in her once again.

"Hi, yourself."

She pulled the sheet up to cover her breasts. "I guess

this is what they call the awkward morning-after moment."

He knew Lori well enough to know that she wasn't the type to jump into bed with just any man. That wasn't the type he needed right now. "The last thing I want to do is make you feel uncomfortable," he said, and leaned toward her. "It's just us, Lori."

She glanced away shyly. "I haven't had a relationship since college."

He found that made him happy. "That's hard to believe." He touched her face. "You're a very beautiful woman, Lorelei Hutchinson."

"Thank you." She glanced away. "I didn't have time for a personal life. Gina and Zack needed me."

"I take it Gina's ex has caused her and you a lot of trouble."

She nodded. "Sober Eric had a mean streak, but when drunk he was really scary. Even with his obvious abuse, it took a lot to convince Gina that the man would never change. Then one day he went after Zack and she finally realized how dangerous he was. That's what it took for her to go to court and testify against him. After that Eric threatened to come after her." Lori's large eyes met his. "That's why it was so hard for me to come to Destiny. When my father made the stipulation in the will about staying a year, I wasn't sure if I could."

"I'm glad you did," he told her, unable to stop touching her. His hand moved over her bare arm, her skin so soft.

She looked surprised. "Is that because I rescued your project?"

"No, it's because you're beautiful and generous." He decided not to fight whatever was going on between them any longer. He leaned down and brushed his mouth over hers, enjoying that she eagerly opened for him. He drew back and added, "You've also taken time with Cassie. Before we moved here she didn't have much female attention."

Lori wasn't sure what she'd expected this morning, but not this. "It's easy to be nice to her. Cassie's a sweet girl."

"Hey, what about me?"

She wrinkled her nose. "I wouldn't call you sweet. Not your disposition anyway."

"Maybe I can change your mind." He caressed her mouth again. "Is that any better?"

"Fishing for a compliment?"

He shifted against her. "How about we continue this without conversation?"

Though Lori wanted the same thing, they needed to get home. "Shouldn't we think about heading back?"

"It's barely dawn." He started working his magic as his mouth moved upward along her jawline. "What's your hurry?" His tongue circled her ear. "Are you trying to get rid of me?"

She gasped, unable to fight the sensation. "No, it's just that it's…" She forgot what she wanted to say as his lips continued along her neck. "Don't we need to leave?"

He raised his head and she could see the desire in his eyes. "I want to do one thing right and it only involves the two of us." He arched an eyebrow. "But if you'd rather go out in that cold weather and start digging out, I'll do it. Your choice."

Lori knew what she wanted, all right. This man. But the fear was that she could never really have him. Last night and these few early hours might be all she would ever have. She wrapped her arms around his neck and pulled his mouth down to hers. "I choose you."

Two hours later, Jace stood at the railing on the cabin porch, drinking coffee. The sun was bright, reflecting off the ten inches of snow covering the ground. The highways would be plowed by now, but not the private road that led to the cabin. He had four-wheel drive on his truck, so they could probably get out and make it to the main road. It better be sooner than later before he got in any deeper.

He had no regrets being with Lori. Making love with her had been incredible. He'd never felt anything like it in his life. Even the best times during his marriage hadn't come close to what he'd shared with Lori.

In just the past three weeks, he'd come to care about this woman more than he had any business doing. But he had strong feelings for Lori and that scared the hell out of him.

Worse, there was no guarantee and he couldn't even offer her a future. He had no extra money. Hell, he needed to rebuild his business. He had to get things settled with the custody issue before he could have a personal life. The question was, would he be able to walk away from Lori? Did he want to?

The front door opened and she stepped out. "I wondered where you went."

"Sorry." He pulled up the collar on her coat and kissed her. "I was just figuring out if we can make it back to town."

"I wouldn't mind getting stuck here a few more days," she admitted. "It's beautiful."

He wouldn't mind pushing reality away for a little

time with this woman. "That would be nice, but we both have jobs to do. Family to take care of."

"Oh, gosh. Gina. I bet she's going crazy with worry."

"Tim called her last night."

"She'll still worry, and be afraid."

Jace wondered who worried about Lori. Seemed she took care of everyone else. "Gina and Zack have Wyatt McCray, Lori. He'll protect them."

"I know," she said with a smile.

His heart began pounding in his chest. The effect she had on him could be a big distraction.

"Thank you for giving us that peace of mind. You've been so kind."

He wondered if she'd always think that. "I didn't do that much."

Those dark eyes locked with his. "You seem to be there whenever I need you."

He found he might not mind being that man. He leaned down to kiss her when he heard something and looked toward the road. "Looks like we're getting rescued."

Jace pointed to a large truck with a plow attached to the front. It stopped a few yards from the door and Toby and Joe climbed out.

Smiling brightly, his foreman called, "I hear someone here might need a ride back to town."

"Toby," Lori cried and hurried down the steps Jace had cleared earlier.

He watched as she ran through the snow to get to Toby. She hugged the big foreman. Jace felt a stab of jealousy stir inside him, but he didn't have any right to claim her. Not yet, maybe never.

* * *

After stopping to get Jace's truck, the ride back to town took about thirty minutes. He followed behind the plow truck until they reached the highway. After Lori gave Toby her car keys, she got into Jace's truck and drove to the Keenan Inn.

She knew she should probably go straight to the house but asked Toby to tow her car to the inn. Besides, she wasn't ready to leave Jace yet.

When they got to the porch, the door opened and they were immediately greeted by Claire and Tim.

"Well, you had yourself quite an adventure," Tim said.

Lori felt a blush rising up her neck as they crossed the threshold. "I guess I should pay better attention to the weather forecast before heading out into the countryside. I did discover my father has a lovely cabin. Thank goodness there was heat."

"Where's Cassie?" Jace asked, looking around.

Claire looked worried. "She's in the kitchen. She's with one of our new guests."

Lori caught Jace's frown. Then he took off and Lori followed him through the dining area and into the large kitchen.

She found Cassie at the counter with a tall, statuesque woman. Her hair was a glossy black in a blunt shoulder-length cut. Her face was flawless, her eyes an azure-blue. She was a beautiful woman until she flashed a hard look at Jace.

The child ran to him. "Daddy. Daddy, you're back."

"Yes, baby." He hugged his daughter. "I told you we got stuck in the snow."

Cassie looked at Lori. "Miss Lori, did you get stuck, too?"

"Yes, your daddy found me."

The child turned back to her father and whispered, "Daddy, don't let Mommy take me away."

Shelly Yeager stood and walked toward them. "Hello, Jace." She gave Lori a once-over. "It's nice to see that you could make it back to take care of our daughter."

"Shelly. What are you doing here?"

"I came to take my little girl home, of course."

An hour later, Lori's car had arrived and she got in and drove home to find a relieved Gina. She'd taken a long shower and gotten dressed in clean clothes, but couldn't push aside the memories from last night. The incredible night she'd shared with Jace, then reality hit them in the face with Shelly Yeager.

She couldn't stop thinking about Cassie and what her mother had said. Was she going to take the child back to Denver? No, Jace couldn't lose his daughter. She wished she could help him, like he'd helped her.

Lori came downstairs to find her sister in the dining room working with Wyatt. The security guard was a retired army man in his forties with buzz-cut hair. She smiled. He didn't look out of place pulling down twenty-year-old brocade drapes. No doubt this wasn't in the man's job description.

Standing back, Maggie was smiling at what was going on. "It's about time someone got rid of those awful things, don't you think?"

"The room does look brighter." Lori had put her sister in charge of making changes to the house. Gina had told her a few days ago about the plans for the dining room. This was good since it had taken her sister's mind off her ex-husband and any trouble he could cause.

Gina finally turned around. "Oh, yes, you look better now. Still a little tired, but better." She walked over as Maggie left the room. "You okay?"

Lori wasn't sure what she was. "I'm fine. We'll talk later." She sighed, not ready to share what had happened with Jace. "So what are you doing in here?"

Her sister smiled. "I hope you don't mind. I decided to take you up on your suggestion and redo the room. I'm going to order some sheer curtains and light-colored linen drapes. Then I'll plan to strip the wallpaper and paint." She went to the sideboard to find the paint chips. "I've narrowed it down to either shaker beige, or winter sunshine."

Lori tried to focus on her sister's selection and push Jace out of her head. It wasn't working. "You're the decorator, you decide."

"Well, since I'm going to keep the woodwork dark, I'm thinking shaker beige." She glanced at Wyatt. "What do you like?"

Lori found herself smiling. At least something was going well today.

"I can do anything I damn well please," Shelly told Jace as she paced her suite upstairs at the inn. Cassie stayed downstairs with the Keenans while her parents talked.

Jace knew better than to get into a fight with this woman. "I thought you wanted me to have Cassie until the first of next year. You were going to be on an extended honeymoon."

Shelly glanced away. "Plans change."

She was hiding something. "So you're going to just rip Cassie out of school and drag her back to Denver? Well, that's as far as you're going, Shelly. You can't take her out of state, and forget about out of the country." He glanced around the large room and into the connecting bedroom. "Where is your so-called duke?"

Shelly glared at him. "His name is Edmund. And he's not a duke." She raised her head as if she was better than everyone. That was always what Shelly wanted to be, but she had come from the same background he had. "He might not be a duke, but he's got money and a bloodline linked to the royal family. And he can take care of me."

That always got to him. He could never make enough money to satisfy her. "I'm happy for you, Shelly. So why are you here and not with…Edmund?"

"There's been a delay in our wedding plans. I might be having second thoughts. So I decided I'd come to see Cassie. And you. You were always good at calming me down."

Something was up with her, and Jace was going to find out what it was. First stop was to visit his lawyer, Paige Keenan Larkin. No one was taking Cassie away from him.

That afternoon, Lori went into her office at the bank. She had to do something to keep her mind off what had happened at the cabin. She also had to think realistically. She couldn't hold out hope about having a future with Jace. His ex-wife showing up in Destiny proved that.

The most important thing she had to remember was that a child was in the middle of this mess. That meant Cassie's welfare had to come first. She had to stay away from Jace Yeager.

A sudden knock brought her back to the present. "Come in."

Jace walked into her office and her breath caught in her throat. Would she ever stop reacting to this man? Her gaze roamed over Jace's six-foot-two frame, recalling how she'd clung to those broad shoulders.

"Lori."

"Jace. What are you doing here?"

"I needed to see you."

Once again she got caught up in his clean-shaven face. Suddenly the memory of his beard stubble moving against her skin caused her to shiver. The sensation had nearly driven her out of her mind.

He closed the door and went to her desk. "I thought we should talk."

She managed a smile, hoping she was covering her insecurities. "There's no need to. Cassie's mother is in town and you need to take care of them. I understand."

"There's nothing to understand except I don't want you caught up in this mess. I have no idea what Shelly is even doing in Destiny. She was supposed to be in England, married and heading off on her honeymoon."

Lori stood. "Did she give you any explanation?"

"Only that plans change," he told her as he crossed the room toward her.

Lori wanted to back away, to tell Jace to leave, that being together now could be dangerous. Instead, she rounded the desk and met him in the middle of the room.

It wasn't planned, but she didn't turn away when his head descended and his mouth captured hers. She surrendered to his eager assault and returned the kiss, hungry for this man. Finally she came to her senses and broke away. "We shouldn't be doing this."

"Are we breaking any laws?"

"But I don't think Shelly was happy when I walked into the inn with you today."

"It's none of her business."

"Jace, you need to get along with her. At least for Cassie's sake."

He pressed his head against hers. "It's funny. Shelly thinks I'm not worthy of her, but she has this need to interfere in my life."

Lori sighed. "I'm so sorry, Jace."

He drew back. "That's the reason I don't want you involved in this fight, Lori. Maybe it would be best if we cool it for a while. I have to think about Cassie."

Lori knew in her head this was the way it had to be, but her heart still ached. She was losing someone she truly cared about. She managed to nod. "Of course. Besides, we both have too much going on to think that far in the future, or at least to make any promises."

This time he looked surprised.

She moved away from him, or he might see how she truly felt. "Come on, Jace. We work together. Last night we gave in to an attraction. It might not have been the wisest thing to do, but it happened."

He studied her a moment. "Are you saying you regret it?"

"That's not the point."

Jace glared at her. The hell it wasn't. He wanted to reach for her, wanted her to admit more than she was. To tell him how incredible their night was. The worst of it was she couldn't do it any more than he could. "You're right."

She nodded. "Goodbye, Jace."

That was the last thing he wanted to hear, but he would only hurt her more if he stayed. He nodded and walked toward the door. It was a lot harder than he ever dreamed it would be, but he couldn't drag Lori into his fight.

CHAPTER TEN

OVER the next three days, Lori felt like she was walking around in a fog. After the incredible night with Jace, then his quick, easy dismissal of it, how could she not? It would be so easy to pull the covers over her head and just stay in bed. If she were living alone she might do just that. Instead she'd stayed home and gotten involved in Gina's redecorating projects. She tried to fill her time with other things, rather than thinking about a tall, dark and handsome contractor.

Then she'd gotten a call from Erin, telling her that Kaley Sims was in town and had agreed to see her. Anxious for the meeting, Lori arrived right at one o'clock and found an attractive woman with short, honey-blond hair and striking gray eyes waiting in her office.

"Ms. Sims. I'm Lori Hutchinson."

Kaley Sims stood up and they shook hands. "It's nice to meet you. And please call me Kaley." The woman studied her and smiled. "I see some resemblance. You have Lyle's eyes." The woman sobered. "I am sorry to hear of his passing."

"Thank you." Lori motioned for Kaley to sit in the chair across from the desk. "I can't tell you how happy

I am that you agreed to meet with me. I see in my files that you worked for my father a few years back."

Kaley nodded. "I was selling real estate in Destiny before he offered me a job as his property manager. I worked for Lyle about three years."

"You managed all his properties?

"I did."

"I'm impressed," Lori said with a smile. "He has a big operation. I can't handle it all, nor do I have the experience to deal with the properties."

Kaley seemed to relax. "I was a single mother, so I needed the money. And the market was different then. Now, property values are a lot lower. You'd lose a fortune selling in this market."

"See, that's something I don't know. You've probably heard that my father left me in charge of all this."

Kaley's eyes widened, then she smiled. "Lyle would be proud. He talked about you a few times."

Lori froze. "He did?" Why did she still want Lyle's approval?

Kaley looked thoughtful. "One day I came in and found him looking at pictures of you. I think you were about eight or nine in the photo. And of course, Destiny being a small town, everyone knew about your parents' divorce. I mentioned to Lyle how cute you were and he should have you come back for a visit. He said he blew his chance."

Lori felt her chest tighten as she fought tears. This wasn't the time to relive the past. She blinked rapidly at the flooding emotions.

Kaley looked panicked. "I'm sorry, I didn't mean to make you sad."

Lori put on a smile, finding she liked this woman.

"You didn't. I never heard anything from my father since the day I left Destiny."

Kaley sighed. "That was Lyle. The only family he had was his father. Poor Billy had lived to be ninety-two and ended up in the nursing home outside of town until his death a few years ago." Kaley studied her. "Do you remember your grandfather?

Lori shook her head. "No, he wasn't around that I recall."

"You were probably lucky. Old Billy boy was what my mother called a hell-raiser. He was one of the last of the miners. Spent his gold as fast as he dug it out. Story has it that he loved gambling and women." Kaley raised an eyebrow. "His exploits were well-known around town. He was nearly broke when he suffered a stroke. It was Lyle who took over running what was left of the family fortune."

"Looks like he did a pretty good job," Lori said.

Kaley nodded in agreement. "I worked for the man, so I know how driven he was." She paused. "I also went with him to visit his father. Old Billy Hutchinson never had a good word to say to his son."

Lori didn't want to get her hopes up that there was something redeeming about Lyle Hutchinson.

Nor did she want to know about any personal relationship her father might have had with Kaley.

She quickly brought herself back to the present. "Well, I didn't ask you to come in to reminisce about my childhood. I was wondering if you'd be interested in coming back here and being my property manager." When Kaley started to speak, Lori stopped her. "I'll double whatever my father paid you."

The woman looked shocked to say the least. "You want me to work for you?"

Lori shook her head. "No, I want you to work *with* me. You have a good business sense, or my father wouldn't have trusted you. The one thing my father didn't offer, I will. There's a place in this company for advancement. Seems the women employees have been overlooked."

Kaley laughed. "I'm sure your father is somewhere cursing your words."

For the first time in two days, Lori laughed. It felt good. "So what do you say, Kaley?"

"I hear around town that you have to stay a year before you get your inheritance. Will you leave after that?"

Lori thought about her sister and nephew. How easily they had adapted to their new life. How Lori herself had, but could she be around Jace knowing she'd never have a life with the man?

She looked at Kaley. "News does travel fast, but no, I want to stay. I care about the residents of Destiny and I want to see the town prosper. Maybe it's my Hutchinson blood, but I can't let the town die away. That's why I need your help. I want to bring more businesses here and create more jobs."

The pretty woman studied her. "I'd like that, too, but there's one thing you need to know about your father and me—"

Lori raised her hand to stop her. "No, I don't need to know anything about your personal life. Makes no difference to me. I only care that you want to work for Hutchinson Corporation." Lori mentioned a yearly salary and benefits.

"Looks like you've got me on your team."

Lori smiled. "How soon can you start?"

"Give me a week to get moved back and get my daughter, Heather, settled in school."

"Let me know if there's anything I can do to help." The phone began to ring. She said goodbye to Kaley then answered.

"Lori Hutchinson."

"Hello, Lori. It's Claire Keenan. I hope I'm not interrupting you."

"Of course not, Claire. What can I do for you?"

"I need a big favor."

Tim Keenan eyed his wife of nearly forty years as she hung up the phone. He knew when she was planning something.

"Okay, what's going on, Claire?"

She turned those gorgeous green eyes toward him. She was also trying to distract him. "Whatever do you mean?"

"I thought you were looking forward to your afternoon volunteering in Ellie's class."

"I was," she admitted. "But I think Lori might need it more. She has to miss teaching. Besides, they're starting the Christmas pageant practice. She's volunteered to help."

Tim arched an eyebrow. "I'd say she has plenty to do taking over for Lyle. What's the real reason?"

"Did you happen to notice Lori and Jace when they were here the other day?"

"You mean after they'd been stranded at the cabin overnight? It was hard not to."

She nodded. "There were several looks exchanged between them." She sighed. "That only proves what

I've known from the moment I saw them together. They would be so perfect for each other, if only they got the chance."

He drew his wife into his arms. Besides her big emerald-green eyes, her loving heart was what drew him to her. The feel of her close still stirred him. "Playing matchmaker again?"

"It's just a little nudge. I'm hoping maybe they'll catch a glimpse of each other when Jace picks up Cassie."

"Sounds good in theory, but what about Shelly Yeager?" He raised his eyes toward the ceiling. The suite on the second floor was still occupied by the ex-wife. "She's been all but shadowing Jace's every move."

A mischievous smile appeared on his bride's lovely face. "I have plans for her."

About four-thirty that afternoon, Jace pulled up at the school and parked his truck. He was tired. More like exhausted ever since Shelly had arrived in town. And she showed no sign of leaving anytime soon. Something was up with her, but he couldn't figure out what it was.

He climbed out of his truck and started toward the auditorium. The last thing he wanted to do was anger his ex so much she'd walk away with Cassie. That was the only reason he'd put up with her dogging him everywhere, including several trips to the construction site. She even showed up at his house most evenings.

He hoped that Paige Larkin would get things in order, and fast, so he could finally go to the judge and stop Shelly's daily threats to take their daughter back to Denver. He liked the fact that Cassie got to spend time with her mother, but only if Shelly didn't end up hurting her.

No, he didn't trust Shelly one bit.

He opened the large door and walked into the theater-style room. Up on stage were several kids along with some teachers giving directions. That was when he caught sight of the petite blonde that haunted his dreams.

He froze as he took in Lori. She had on dark slacks and a gray sweater that revealed her curves and small waist. He closed his eyes and could see her lying naked on the big bed, her hair spread out on the pillow, her arms open wide to him.

He released a long breath. As much as he'd tried to forget Lori, she wouldn't leave his head, or his heart. All right, he'd come to care about her, but that didn't mean he could do anything about it.

The rehearsal ended and his daughter came running toward him. "Daddy! Daddy!" She ran into his arms and hugged him. "Did you see me practice?"

He loved seeing her enthusiasm. "I sure did."

Jace glanced up to see Lori coming toward them. His heart thudded in his chest as his gaze ate her up. Those dark eyes, her bright smile. His attention went to her mouth as he recalled how sweet she tasted. He quickly pulled himself back to the present, realizing the direction of his thoughts.

"Hello, Lori."

Her gaze avoided his. "Hi, Jace."

"Looks like you've got your hands full here."

"I don't mind at all. I love working with the kids. I gladly volunteered."

Why couldn't he have met this woman years ago?

Cassie drew his attention back to her. "Daddy, did you know that our play is called *Destiny's First Christmas?* It's about Lori's great-great grandfather Raymond Hutchinson. On Christmas Eve, he was working in his mine, 'The Lucky Strike,' and found gold. That night he made a promise to his wife to build a town."

Jace looked at Lori. "Not exactly the traditional Christmas story."

She shrugged. "Not my choice, but the kids voted to do this one. Probably because of my father's passing."

"No, I'd say because of you. You've made a lot of positive changes in the last month."

She shook her head. "Just trying to bring Lyle Hutchinson's business practices into the new century."

Jace found he didn't want to leave, but he couldn't keep staring at her and remembering how it was to hold her in his arms and make love to her.

Cassie tugged on his coat sleeve. "Daddy, I forgot to tell you, Miss Lori invited us to her house for Thanksgiving."

That surprised Jace.

"She's invited a whole bunch of people. It's going to be a big party. Can we go?"

The last thing he wanted to do was disappoint his daughter. "We'll talk about it. Why don't you go get your books." After he sent Cassie off, he turned back to Lori. "Please, don't feel you have to invite us."

"I don't. I wanted to invite you and Cassie, Jace. Besides, practically everyone else in town is coming. The Keenans and Erin and her family. A lot of the bank employees." She glanced away, not meeting his eyes. "And I plan to extend the invitation to Toby and the

construction crew. There's going to be a lot of people
at the house. I did it mainly for Gina and Zack so they
could meet everyone. So you and Cassie are welcome."

Jace wanted so badly to reach out and touch her. He
told himself that would be enough, but that was a lie.
He wanted her like he'd never wanted a woman ever.
"If you're sure."

She frowned. "Of course. We're business partners."

And that was all they could be, he thought. "Speaking
of that, you need to come by the site. We're down to
doing the finish trim work and adding fixtures. I'd like
your opinion on how things are turning out."

She nodded. "How soon to completion?"

"Toby estimates two weeks."

"That's great. Then we can concentrate on getting
the spaces rented. I can help with that since I've hired
a property manager, Kaley Sims. If it's okay with you,
I'd like her to come by and talk with you about listing
the loft apartments."

Jace smiled. "So she's handling the rest of your properties?"

Lori nodded. "Yes, she worked for my father years
ago, so she knows what she's doing. I convinced her to
come back to work with me."

"Good, I'm ready to get this done."

She stiffened. "And you don't have to deal with a
rookie partner."

He cursed. "Ah, Lori, I didn't mean it that way. It's
just with all the delays we've had, I'm ready to be finished. You're a great partner. I'd work with you again."

She looked surprised. "You would?"

"In a heartbeat." He took a step toward her. There
was so much he wanted to say, but he had no right to

make promises when he wasn't sure what was in store for him and Cassie. He was in the middle of a messy custody battle. "Just come by the site tomorrow."

Lori started to speak when he heard his name called. He turned around to find Shelly coming toward him. Great. He didn't need this.

He turned back around but Lori had walked off. He wanted to go after her, but he couldn't, not until he got things settled. He'd better do it quickly, or he might lose one of the best things that ever happened to him.

The next week, Lori did what Jace asked and came by the site. She'd purposely stayed away from the project to avoid the man, so she was amazed at the difference.

The chain-link fence had been removed. They'd already started to do some stone landscape. Planters and retaining walls had been built, and a parking area.

"I'm impressed," Kaley said as she got out of the car and looked at the two-story wood-and-stone structure.

So was Lori. "Wait until you see the inside."

They headed up the path to the double-door entry. The door swung open and Toby greeted them with a big smile.

"Well, it's about time you showed up again."

Lori returned the smile. "Well, I knew you were in charge so I didn't worry about things getting done. Hello, Toby."

After a greeting, the foreman turned to Kaley and grinned. "Well, well, who's your friend, Lori?"

Lori made the introductions. "Kaley Sims, Hutchinson Corp's property manager, Toby Edwards."

"So you're not just a pretty face," Toby said.

"And you'd be wise to remember that, Mr. Edwards."

She took a step toward him, grinning. "Now, let's go see if this place looks as good as Lori says it does."

"Well, damn. You're making my day brighter and brighter."

Lori was surprised to see these two throw off sparks. "Go on ahead and don't mind me," she called as the two took off, not paying any attention to her.

She stepped through the entry and gasped as she looked around. The dark hardwood floors had been laid and the massive fireplace completed. She eyed the golden tones of the stacked stones that ran all the way from the hearth to the open-beam ceiling.

Then her attention went to the main attraction of the huge room. The arching staircase. The new design was an improvement from the old as the natural wood banister wrapped around the edge of the first floor, showing off the mezzanine. A front desk had been built for a receptionist for the tenants.

"So how do you like it so far?"

Lori swung around to see Jace. "It looks wonderful."

Then she took in the man. In his usual uniform of faded jeans and a dark Henley shirt, Jace also wore a carpenter's tool belt around his waist. Somehow that even looked sexy.

"Am I disturbing your work?"

He grinned. "Darlin', you've been disturbing a lot more than my work since the minute I met you."

Jace was in a good mood today. Although Shelly had no plans to leave town, he had talked to Paige first thing that morning. He now had a court date and also a preliminary injunction so Shelly couldn't run off with Cassie. At least not until after the custody hearing back in Denver.

"We butted heads a lot, too," she said.

He leaned forward and breathed, "And there were times when we couldn't keep our hands off each other." Before she could do more than gasp, he took her hand. "Come on, I want to show you around."

"I need to go with Toby and Kaley."

He led her up the staircase. "I think Toby can handle the job." He took her into the first loft apartment, showing off ebony-colored hardwood floors. The open kitchen had dark-colored cabinets, but the counters weren't installed yet. "Here are some granite samples for the countertops and tile for the backsplash."

He watched her study the light-colored granite, with the earth-toned contrasting tile. The other was a glossy black, with white subway tile. "I like the earth tone," she told him.

He smiled. "My choice, too. The next stop is the bathroom." He led her across the main living space, where the floor-to-ceiling windows stopped her.

"Oh, Jace. This is a wonderful view."

He stood behind her, careful not to touch her as they glanced out the window at the San Juan Mountains. He worked hard to concentrate on the snow-filled creases in the rock formations and evergreen trees dotting the landscape. "It's almost as beautiful as the view from the cabin."

She glanced up at him and he saw the longing in her dark eyes. "It was lovely there, wasn't it?"

"You were even more beautiful, Lori."

She shook her head. "Don't, Jace. We decided that we shouldn't be involved."

"What if I can't stay away from you?"

Lori closed her eyes. She didn't want to hope and be

hurt in the end. Then his mouth closed over hers and she lost all reasonable thoughts. With a whimper of need she moved her hands up his chest and around his neck and gave in to the feelings.

He broke off the kiss. "I've missed you, Lori. I missed holding you, touching you, kissing you."

"Jace…"

His mouth found hers again and again.

Finally the sound of voices broke them apart. His gaze searched her face. "Lucky for you we're not alone. I'm pretty close to losing control." He sighed. "And with you, Lorelei Hutchinson, that happens every time I get close." He pulled her against him so there was no doubt. "Please, say you'll come by the house tonight. There are so many things I want to tell you."

Lori wanted to hope that everything would work out with Jace. Yet, still Shelly Yeager lingered in town. The last thing Lori wanted was to jeopardize Jace getting custody of his daughter.

Yet, she wanted them both—Jace and Cassie—in her life. Question was, was she ready to fight for what she wanted? Yes. "What time?"

CHAPTER ELEVEN

AT THE site, Jace kept checking his watch, but it was only two o'clock. He had three more hours before he could call it a day and see Lori again.

He was crazy to add any more complications to his life, but he hadn't been able to get her out of his head. For weeks, he'd tried to deny his feelings, tried to convince himself that he didn't care about Lori, but he did care. A lot.

He hadn't been able to forget her or what happened between them. The night at the cabin, what they'd shared, made him think it was possible to have a relationship again. Tonight, when she came by the house, he planned to tell her. He only hoped she could be patient and hang in there a little while longer, until this custody mess was finally straightened out.

"Hey, are you listening?"

Jace turned toward his friend Justin Hilliard. "Sorry, what did you say?"

Justin smiled. "Seems you have something or someone else on your mind."

"Yeah, I do. But I can't do anything about it right now so I'd rather not talk about it."

"I understand. If you need a friend to talk later, I'm your guy. I'll even buy the beer."

Justin was the one who'd brought him to Destiny after Yeager Construction tanked following his divorce. He'd always be grateful. "I appreciate that."

His friend nodded. "Now, tell me when can I move in?" He motioned around the office space on the main floor at the Mountain Heritage complex.

"Is next week soon enough?"

"Great. I'll have Morgan go shopping for office furniture. And I'll need a loft apartment upstairs for out-of-town clients. Is there someone handling the loft rentals?"

Jace nodded. "Kaley Sims. I'll have her get in touch with you to negotiate the lease."

"Good. I'm available all this week." Justin studied Jace. "So what are your plans for your next project?"

"Not sure." That much was true. "I've been so wrapped up in getting this project completed, I haven't thought that far ahead." He had Lori on his mind. "I know I'd like to stay here, of course, but until I get this custody mess taken care of, I'm still in limbo."

"Like I said, let me know if I can help." Justin slapped him on the back. "Just don't let Shelly get away with anything."

"Believe me, I won't." She'd taken him to the cleaners once. No more. "Besides, Paige is handling it all for me."

Justin nodded. "Yeah, my sister-in-law is one of the best. She'll do everything she can to straighten this out."

God, he hoped so. Jace wanted nothing more than to end Shelly's threats.

They walked out of the office space and Justin said, "If you think you'd be ready to start another project by March, let me know."

Jace stopped. He was definitely interested. "What kind of project?"

"It's an idea I've had in the works awhile. I waited until I had the right partner in place, and now, it's in the designing stages."

Jace was more than intrigued. "So what is it?"

"A mountain bike racing school and trails. I bought several acres of land about five miles outside of town and plan to build a track. I'm bringing in a pro racer, Ryan Donnelly, to design it."

"I don't do landscaping."

Justin smiled. "I know. I want your company to handle the structures, cabins to house the students and instructors, including a main building to serve meals and a pro shop."

They walked through the main area of the building as Justin continued. "Eventually, I hope to work with Ryan to design bikes. I want the plant to be right here in Destiny." Justin arched an eyebrow. "I want you to handle it all, Jace."

This was a dream come true. "And I want the project, Justin. By early spring I could have the subs and crew in place to start." He worked to hold in his excitement. "But I'll need the plans by February."

Justin nodded. "Shouldn't be a problem."

Now if his personal life straightened out by then. With this new project he could move forward, make a fresh start. He thought about Lori. He couldn't wait to tell her. Tonight. This could be their new beginning.

* * *

By six o'clock, Lori had gathered her things and left the office. She went home, showered and changed into a nice pair of slacks and white angora sweater. Excited about spending the evening with Jace, she took extra time with her clothes and makeup.

Her pulse raced as she realized how badly she wanted to be with him. He was everything she'd ever dreamed the man she loved could be. Handsome, caring and a good father. What woman wouldn't dream about forever with him?

She walked back into the connecting bedroom to find Gina.

"Sorry, Lori, I didn't mean to disturb you. I know you plan to go out tonight."

"You never could disturb me," Lori assured her sister. "Is something wrong?"

Gina smiled. "No. For the first time in a very long time, everything is going right." She went to her sister. "Thanks to you. I never thought I could feel this happy again. And Zack…"

Lori hugged her, praying that continued. That Eric would leave them alone. "We're family, Gina. Besides, it's Lyle's money."

"No, you were there for us long before you inherited the Hutchinson money. You were always there for me."

"You're my sister and Zack is my nephew. Where else would I be?"

"Having a life?" Gina said. "And finding someone special."

Lori wanted to believe. "I think that has already happened."

Her sister smiled. "If Jace Yeager is as smart as I think he is, he'll snatch you up."

Of course, Lori hoped that tonight the man would make some kind of commitment, but she also knew he had to tread cautiously. They both did. "Let's just see what happens."

About eight o'clock that evening, Jace had put Cassie to bed, but she made him promise when Lori got there she would come up to say good-night. He was happy that his daughter got along with her.

He smiled, knowing he'd have Lori all to himself for the rest of the evening. There were so many things he wanted to tell Lori tonight. He wanted them to move ahead together.

He checked on the dinners he'd picked up from the Silver Spoon. Then he took the wine out of the refrigerator and got two glasses from the cupboard. He looked around his half-finished kitchen.

Okay, this place had been neglected too long. It was going to be his top priority. He could probably make some headway by Christmas. Thanksgiving at the Hutchinson house, and maybe, Christmas dinner at the Yeager house. That would be his goal.

He hoped to have the rest of his life in order by then, too. His daughter with him and Lori with them. He'd made a start with the custody hearing.

He saw the flash of headlights as a car pulled into the drive. His heart began to pound when he saw Lori climb out and walk up the steps to the back porch. He opened the door and greeted her with a smile.

"Hi, there."

She smiled. "Hi. Sorry I'm late."

Jace drew her into his arms because he couldn't go any longer without touching her, holding her. "Well, you're here now and that's all that matters. I missed you." He kissed her, a slow but intense meeting of their mouths, only making him hungry for more.

He didn't want to let go of her, but he promised himself he'd go slow. He tore his mouth away. "Maybe we should dial it down a little." He tugged at her heavy coat. "At least until I feed you."

She smiled. "I am a little hungry." She brushed her hair back and looked around. "Where's Cassie?"

"I'm losing out to the kid, huh? She's upstairs in bed." He led her into the kitchen. "I told her you'd come up and say good-night. I hope you don't mind."

"Of course not." Lori started off, but he brought her back to him for another intense kiss. "Just remember you're mine for the rest of the night."

"I'll be right back."

Jace's heart pounded as he watched the cute sway of her hips as she walked out of the kitchen and up the stairs.

He sighed and worked to get it together. "You got it bad, Yeager." He turned down the lights, and put on some music from the sound system, then lit the candles on the table. Back at the kitchen counter, he opened the chilled bottle of wine and filled the glasses at the two place settings.

It was impossible not to remember their dinner together at the cabin. He wanted nothing more than to have a repeat of that night. But that couldn't happen. Not with Cassie here. He blew out a breath. There was no doubt in his mind, they'd be together again. And soon.

Smiling, Lori walked down the steps and it turned into a grin when she saw Jace in the kitchen. "That's what I like about you, Yeager. You're just not a handsome face, you're domestic, too."

Jace turned around and tossed her a sexy smile. "I can be whatever you want."

Her heart shot off racing. *How about the man who loves me?* she asked silently as he came to her and drew her against him. She wanted nothing more than to stay wrapped in his arms, to close out the rest of the world.

She looked up at him. "Kiss me, Jace."

"My pleasure, ma'am." He lowered his head, brushing her mouth with his. She opened for him, but he was a little more playful and took nibbling bites out of her bottom lip.

With her whimper of need, he captured her mouth in a searing kiss. By the time he pulled back, her knees were weak and she had trouble catching her breath. "Wow."

He raised an eyebrow. "That was just an appetizer." He stepped back. "But before I go back to sampling you again, we better eat."

She was a little disappointed, but knew it was better to slow things down a little. She accepted the wine he offered her.

She sipped it and let the sweet taste linger in her mouth. She caught Jace watching her and smiled, then took another sip. "How was your day at the site?"

"Oh, I meant to tell you that Justin stopped by. Besides the office space, he wants to lease a loft apartment. I gave him Kaley's number."

"Good." She raised her glass. "The first of many, I hope."

"You and me both. Justin might want more than one apartment. I'm hoping Kaley can convince him of that.

Maybe give him a few incentives like a six-month re-
duction in the rent."

"That sounds good. Is that usually done in real estate?"

He nodded. "All the time." He walked her to the table
and sat her down, then began filling their plates with
roast chicken and mashed potatoes. "The Silver Spoon's
Thursday night special."

Lori took a bite. "It's very good."

"Come spring," he began, "I'll barbecue us some
steaks on the grill. That's my specialty."

She paused, her fork to her mouth. He was talking
about the future. "I'd like that."

He winked and took a bite of food as they continued
to talk about Mountain Heritage, then he told her about
Justin's offer for the racing bike school.

"Oh, Jace, you have to be excited about that."

Jace wanted to be, but there were still problems
looming overhead. Like getting permanent custody of
his daughter. He prayed that Paige could pull this off.
"There's still a lot to work out."

Lori nodded.

He didn't want to talk about it right now. This was
just for them. No troubles, no worries, just them. Yet,
he knew he couldn't make her any promises. He'd never
thought he'd find someone like Lori, someone he'd want
to dream about a future together.

The meal finished, they carried the dishes to the sink
and left them. He offered her coffee, but she refused it.

A soft ballad came on the radio. He drew her into his
arms and began slowly dancing her around the kitchen
and into the family room, where soft flames in the fireplace added to the mood. He placed his hands against

her back, pulling his swaying body against hers. "I want you, Lori," he whispered. "Never have I wanted a woman as much as you." His lips trailed along her jaw, feeling her shiver. He finally reached his destination. "Never." He closed his mouth over hers, and pushed his tongue inside tasting her, stroking her.

His hands were busy, too, reaching under her sweater, cupping her breasts.

"Jace," she moaned. "Please."

"I definitely want to please you." He kissed her again and was quickly getting to the point of no return.

"Well, well. Isn't this cozy?"

Jace jerked back and caught sight of Shelly standing in the doorway. He immediately turned Lori away from view. "What are you doing here?"

The tall brunette pushed away from the doorjamb and walked into the room as if she had every right to be there.

"Since no one was answering the phone, I came to see what the problem was." She gave Lori a once-over. "Now I know why. You're having a little party here while our daughter is asleep upstairs."

"That's my business, Shelly. And that doesn't give you the right to come into my house without an invitation. And you weren't invited."

"I don't need to be. I have custody of Cassie." She shot an angry look at Lori. "In fact I think I should remove her from here right now."

Lori gasped.

Jace got angry. "I wouldn't try it, Shelly."

"Try and stop me."

When she started to move past him, Jace stepped in

front of her. "You can't. I have an injunction that says she stays with me until the court hearing."

She glared. "I know. I got served today."

So that was why she showed up. "And this should be settled in court."

"I want my daughter. Now!"

"Stop it! Mommy, Daddy, don't fight!"

They all turned and saw Cassie standing at the bottom of the stairs.

Lori wanted to go to the child, but it wasn't her place.

Jace took over and went to his daughter's side. "Oh, baby. I'm sorry we woke you."

"You and Mommy were fighting again?"

"I'm sorry. We're trying to work something out and we got a little loud."

"Please, I don't want you to fight anymore."

Jace looked at Lori. "Will you take Cassie back to her room?" With her nod, he glanced down at his daughter. "I'll be up in a minute."

Shelly came over and kissed her daughter and sent her along.

Once they were alone, Jace took Shelly's arm and walked her out to the utility room. "I'm not going to let you come here and upset Cassie like that."

"You're just mad because I interrupted your rendezvous with little Miss Heiress."

"Leave Lori out of this. She's a respectable person in this town."

"And you're sleeping with her."

Jace had to hold his temper. "We've done nothing wrong. If you think so, then talk to the judge. I'll see you in court, Shelly."

Shelly's face reddened in anger. "Don't think you've

won, Jace Yeager. This is not going to end in your favor."

He held on to his temper. "Why, Shelly? Why are we arguing about this? You know Cassie is better off here. She's made friends and is doing great in school. I have a job that has me home every night." He stopped in front of the woman he once loved, but now he only felt sorry for. "When you get married, Shelly, I will let you see her anytime you want."

"That might not happen. So the game plan will change."

"Oh, Cassie."

Lori cradled the small form against her as they sat on the bed. She inhaled the soft powdery smell and realized how much Cassie had come to mean to her. She could easily become addicted to this nightly ritual.

She silently cursed Shelly Yeager. How could anyone drag a child into this mess? "I wish I could make it better, sweetheart."

The child's lip quivered as she looked up. "Nobody can. They always fight."

"I'm sorry. That doesn't mean they don't love you. They just have to work out what's best for you."

A tear ran down the girl's cheek. "I want to live here with Daddy, but if I do, Mommy will go away." Cassie's big blue eyes looked up at her, and Lori could feel her pain. "And she's gonna forget about me." She started to sob and Lori drew her into a tight embrace.

"Oh, sweetheart, have you told your father how you feel?"

The child pulled back, looking panicked. "No! I don't

want them to fight anymore." Her face crumpled again. "So please don't tell Daddy."

"Don't tell me what?"

They both looked toward the door to see Jace. "Nothing." Cassie wiped her eyes. "I'm just talking to Miss Lori."

Lori got up and Jace sat down to face his daughter. "Sweetheart, I'm sorry."

The little girl suddenly collapsed into her father's arms. Lori backed out of the room, not wanting to intrude. She realized right away how much this custody battle had affected the child.

And Cassie had to come first.

Lori couldn't help but wonder if they could get through this situation unscathed, or would Shelly follow through on her threats?

Lori's chest tightened. She'd never forget the heartache she'd felt when she had to leave her childhood home. Her father standing on the porch. That had been the last time she'd ever seen Lyle Hutchinson. Oh, God. She couldn't let that happen to this little girl. No matter what it cost her.

Cassie finally went to sleep and Jace walked out into the hall, but he didn't go downstairs yet. Heartsick over his daughter's distress, he needed some time to pull himself together. Cassie had been dealing with problems he and her mother had caused. No child should have to choose which parent to love, which parent to be loyal to.

He sighed, knowing he had to do something about it.

Jace made his way down the steps and found Lori standing in the kitchen. He went to her and pulled her into a tight embrace. "I guess we should talk." He released her and walked around the kitchen in a daze. "You want something to drink?"

"No," she said. "Is Cassie asleep?"

He nodded, feeling the rush of emotions as he went and poured himself a glass. "I'm so angry at Shelly for starting all this."

"Divorce isn't easy for anyone, kids especially." Lori closed her eyes momentarily. "Cassie needs constant re-assurance that her daddy's going to be around."

Jace tried to draw a breath, but it was hard. "And I have been right here for her. I've been doing everything possible to keep her with me."

He immediately realized the harshness of his words. "I'm sorry, Lori, that you had to witness this." He pulled her close, grateful that she didn't resist. "I'm so frus-trated." He held her tightly. "I've worked so hard to have a good relationship with my daughter."

Lori pulled back, knowing there wasn't any sim-ple solution. "I know, but Cassie is still caught in the middle."

"This is all a game to Shelly."

It wasn't for the rest of the people involved. "Well, she is here and you have to deal with her. For Cassie's sake."

"I've been doing that," he told her. "Paige has got-ten a court date for a custody hearing with a judge in Denver."

Lori was surprised by Jace's news. "That's good. When?"

"This coming Monday."

She told herself not to react, not to be hurt that he hadn't said anything before now. "So soon?"

He studied her with those intense blue eyes. "If we

don't do it now, the holidays are coming up. It could be delayed until January. By then Shelly might have taken Cassie to Europe." He paused. "I was going to tell you about it tonight."

That didn't take away the pain of his leaving. "How long will you be gone?"

"Probably just a few days. Don't worry, Toby has the project under control."

She shook her head. "You think I'm concerned about that when Cassie's future is in jeopardy?"

He shook his head. "Of course not, Lori. I know you care about her."

"I care about both of you. I want this to work, because she should be with you."

He looked at her, his blue eyes intense. "I'm going to see that happens no matter what the judge's decision is."

Lori felt her heart skip a beat. "Does that mean you'll move back to Denver?"

He nodded slowly. "I hope there's another way. I don't want to leave here, but if that's the end result of this hearing…there's no choice."

He might be going away, she thought, fighting tears. "Cassie's your daughter, so of course you have to go there. You have to fight for her."

"I care about you, Lori. A lot. I know you have a year commitment here, or I'd ask—"

"Then don't, Jace," she interrupted, forcing a smile. "Neither one of us is ready to jump into a relationship. Like you said, we both have other commitments."

His gaze locked on hers. "I want to say the hell with all of Shelly's games, but I can't. Bottom line is, I can't give you any promises."

And she couldn't beg him to. There was too much

at stake here. Most importantly, a little girl. Lori had once been that little girl whose father let her go. Cassie deserved better.

Lori couldn't meet his eyes. She fisted her hands so he wouldn't see her shaking. "It's too soon to make plans when we don't know the future."

"Is it? What about what happened between us at the cabin? Unless it didn't mean anything to you."

She swallowed hard. "Of course it did." She'd always have those incredible memories. "It was…special."

"Seems not as special for you as it was for me."

She had to get away from him. "I'm sorry, Jace. I need to go. I hope everything works out for you and Cassie." She headed toward the door and paused. She took one last look at the man she loved. "Goodbye, Jace."

When he didn't say anything to stop her, she hurried out the door and got into her car. Starting the engine, she headed for the highway. He hadn't even asked her to wait it out. Tears filled her eyes, blurring her vision, until she had to stop.

She cried for her loss, for letting this between her and Jace to get this far. She never should have let herself fall in love with this wonderful man. A man she couldn't have. She'd finally opened herself and let love in, only to be hurt again.

She brushed away more tears, praying that the pain would stop. That the loneliness would go away soon. This was what she got for starting to dream of that happy ending.

The only consolation was she wouldn't let another little girl go through the misery she had. She would never prevent Jace from having his daughter.

CHAPTER TWELVE

THAT night, sleep eluded Lori.

When she'd gotten home earlier she'd made up an excuse to go to her room. She hadn't been in the mood to talk about her evening with Jace. Not even with Gina. And what good would it do? Neither one of them had a choice in the matter. There was nothing to say except they couldn't be together.

But after several hours of tossing and turning, she got out of bed. Restless, she ended up wandering around the big house. She checked in on her sleeping nephew and pulled the covers around him, knowing Jace would do the same thing with Cassie. Smiling, she realized that had been one of the reasons she'd fallen in love with the man. His relationship with his daughter was part of that. She would miss them both so much if they couldn't come back here. What were Jace's chances of getting custody? Probably slim.

Lori walked down the hall, passing her childhood bedroom. She stopped, wanting nothing more than to shake the feeling of abandonment she'd had since her mother took her away from here.

She slipped inside, waiting as the moonlight coming through the window lit her path to the canopy bed.

Loneliness swept through her as more memories flooded back. Her absent father had been too busy for her. He'd been too busy making money and that meant he hadn't been home much.

Then long-forgotten images flashed though her mind. There had been some happy times. She remembered sitting at the dinner table, hearing her parents' laughter. Lyle wasn't very demonstrative, but she would always cherish the time he'd spent with her. Guess he'd been as loving as he was able to be.

She smiled, thinking of those good-night kisses she would treasure. She brushed away a tear as she turned on a bedside lamp and caught sight of the stuffed animals lined up on the windowsill.

Another memory hit her. "Oh, Daddy, you gave me all of these."

"Lorelei?"

Lori turned to find Maggie standing in the doorway. She was wearing her robe over a long gown. "Oh, Maggie, did I wake you?"

The housekeeper walked in. "No, I was up getting something to drink. This old house has a lot creaks and I know them all. When I heard someone walking around, I thought it might be the boy." The older woman eyed the stuffed animals. "Land sakes, child. You can't keep coming in here and getting all sad."

"No, Maggie. Really, I'm fine." She smiled as she wiped away the tears and held out one of her childhood animals. "Look. I remembered that Dad bought this for me." She reached for another. "He bought these, too." She gathered all them in her arms.

Maggie smiled. "I'm glad you remember those times."

And so much more. "Every time he went on a business trip, he came home with a toy for me." Another memory. "And when he was home he would come into my bedroom and kiss me good-night." Tears flooded her eyes. "He loved me, Maggie."

"Of course he loved you. You were his little girl, his pride and joy."

"Then why, Maggie? Why didn't he want me?"

The housekeeper shook her head. "It wasn't that." She hesitated, then said, "You never knew your grandfather Billy. If you had you might understand your father better."

"Kaley Sims mentioned him. She said he'd gone into a nursing home after a stroke."

Maggie made a huffing sound. "It was probably better than he deserved. That man was a terrible example as a parent. What Lyle went through as a child was... Let's just say, Billy wasn't much of a human being, so I won't go into his fathering skills."

"Wouldn't that make Lyle a better one?"

Maggie took hold of Lori's hands and they sank down to sit on the window seat. "I believe your dad did the best he could, honey. When Billy nearly lost all the family money, and that included the bank, this town almost didn't survive. Your father spent a lot of years rebuilding the family wealth, and trying to get Billy's approval."

Maggie continued, "Your mother didn't like being neglected, either. She wanted all of her husband's attention. I think she left hoping Lyle would come after both of you. Your father took it as another rejection and just shut down."

Lori had no doubt Jocelyn Hutchinson would do that to get attention. "But he had a daughter who loved him."

Maggie looked sad. "I know. I wish I had a better answer for you. I recall a few phone conversations between your mother and father. He asked Jocelyn to bring you here. She refused. When your mother remarried, he told me that you'd do better without him."

She felt a spark of hope. "He wanted me to come back here?"

Maggie nodded. "For Christmas that first year. He told me once how much you loved the tree lights in the town square."

A tear ran down Lori's cheek. She had no idea he would remember.

Maggie pulled her into a comforting embrace. "He kept this room the same, hoping to have you back here. So keep hanging on to the good memories, child. I know that was what your father did."

Lori pulled back. "How can I?"

The housekeeper brushed back Lori's hair. "Because your father knew he caused enough pain over the years." Maggie smiled through her own tears. "Think about it, Lorelei. Your father finally brought you home. No mistaking, he wanted you here."

Lori began to sob over the lost years that father and daughter would never get back. The tears were cleansing, and she had some answers.

"Lori?"

Lori looked at the open door to find her sister. "Oh, Gina. Sorry, did we wake you?"

"I was just checking on Zack."

Maggie hugged them both. "Share with your sister, Lorelei. It will get better each time." The older woman left.

"Should I be worried?" Gina asked once they were alone.

"Not any longer. I've learned a lot about my father. Lyle wasn't perfect, but he loved me in his way." Lori went on to explain about her discovery.

"I'm so glad," Gina agreed. "Every child needs those good memories." She hesitated. "That's what I hope for Zack."

"He'll have those good memories. I promise," Lori told her, thinking about Cassie, too.

Lori never wanted that child to go through what she had. So that meant she had to accept it. Accept she might not be able to have Jace Yeager.

Gina's voice broke into her thoughts.

Lori looked at her. "What?"

"Something else is bothering you. Would it have anything to do with Jace? Did you two have a fight?" Gina asked, frowning. "Oh, no, it's his ex-wife causing trouble, isn't it?"

Lori agreed. "Jace has to go back to Denver for the custody case. If he loses, he wants to live close by Cassie. That means he'll have to move back there."

"I wish I could hate the guy, but he's a great father." Gina suddenly grinned. "So move to Denver."

Lori would in a minute. "I can't until I fulfill Lyle's will. If I leave before the year is up, the town might not survive."

"That doesn't mean you can't go visit Jace for long weekends."

She could go for that. Would Jace want a long-distance relationship? "He hasn't asked me."

Gina jumped up. "Of course he hasn't. He doesn't know anything yet. Lori, I believe Jace Yeager loves you. And if he can, he'll do whatever it takes to get Cassie and come back here to you."

Lori was heartened with her sister's enthusiasm. "You sure seem to have a better outlook toward men these days."

Her sister shrugged. "Maybe they aren't all jerks like Eric. I've met a few here in town that seem really nice. Now, that doesn't mean I want to get involved with any of them. I'm happy concentrating on raising Zack."

If one good thing came out of returning to Destiny it was helping Gina and Zack have a chance at a new life. "And we have each other."

"Always." Gina nodded. "Now, we need something to do to keep you busy." She looked around what once had been a little girl's room. "This entire house, at the very least, needs a fresh coat of paint. We should re-decorate the master suite, so you can move in there."

Lori knew Gina was trying to distract her, and she loved her for it. "The place is a little big for us, don't you think?"

"Of course it is. It's a mansion."

Lori turned to her sister. "What about moving into a smaller place?"

Her sister blinked. "Are you going to sell this house?"

She shook her head. "We have to live here for now. I think maybe Hutchinson House can be rented out for weddings and parties and the proceeds could go to the town." She couldn't help but wonder if Jace and Cassie would be living here in Destiny, too. "What do you think of that?"

"Lori, I think that's a wonderful idea." She hesitated.

"And you've been generous to Zack and me. But I feel I need to contribute, too. I know this mess with Eric still has me frightened, but thanks to you, I've felt safer than I have for years."

"I'm glad." Lori had already checked on her ex-brother-in-law. She'd contacted the police detective on the case. Eric had been staying with his family in Colorado Springs.

"I need a job," Gina blurted out. "It's not that I'm not grateful to you for everything, but I want to be more independent. I have to set a good example for my son. I don't want him to think he has an easy ride in life."

Lori hugged her, knowing the hell she'd gone through for years. "So you want a job. I just happen to have one."

Her sister frowned. "Lori, you can't make up a job for me."

"I hate to tell you, sis, but most of the people in Destiny work for Hutchinson Corp. And honestly, I'm not making this job up. Kaley Sims is going to advertise the Mountain Heritage spaces to rent and she needs to stage them. You're the perfect decorator to do it. So what do you say?"

Gina gave her a big smile. "I say, when do I start?"

"I'll talk to Kaley in the morning." Lori smiled, but inside she was hurting. Everyone was moving forward, but she couldn't, not knowing what her future held. "Come on, we both need to get some sleep."

They walked back to their rooms. Lori climbed in bed just as her cell phone rang. She reached for it off her nightstand.

She glanced at the familiar caller ID. "Jace," she answered. "Is something wrong?"

"No, nothing's wrong. I'm sorry I called so late. I just wanted to let you know that Cassie and I are leaving."

She already knew that. "When?"

"First thing in the morning."

So soon.

Jace went on. "Toby has everything under control at the site. There are only a few finishing touches before the last walk through. Kaley Sims is now handling the Heritage project. I'll pass on the news to her."

"I appreciate that," she told him. "Is there anything else?"

Lori begged silently that he'd ask her to wait for him. At least tell her he cared.

"I hated the way we left things last night," he finally said. "God, Lori, I wish it could be different."

She swallowed back the lump in her throat. "You're doing what's right, Jace."

"I know. I just needed to hear your voice," he told her and there was a long pause. "Goodbye, Lori." Then he hung up.

The silence was deafening. She lay back in her bed, pulling up the covers to protect her from the loneliness. It didn't help. Nothing would help but Jace.

"Why are you dead set on making my life hell?" Jace demanded as he stepped through the door into his one-time Denver home the next day. Something else that Shelly had gotten from their divorce.

He glanced around the spacious entry of the re-furbished Victorian. The hardwood floors he'd refin-ished himself, along with the plaster on the walls. He stopped the search when unpleasant memories of his marriage hit him. He turned back to Shelly to see her stubborn look.

"You're the one who had me served with papers."

"Because you came to Destiny and disrupted Cassie's life. I'm done with your games, Shelly. It's time we settle this."

"Well, that's too bad." She strolled across the room to the three windows that overlooked the street. "I'm Cassie's mother, and after today, the judge will see that I should have our child permanently. Where is our daughter?"

"She's in good hands." Paige had offered to watch her back at the hotel while he tried to straighten out a few things. "She's with Paige Larkin."

Shelly frowned. "So what are you willing to give up to spend time with Cassie? Your little girlfriend?"

"I'm not willing to give up anything. Besides, my personal life is none of your business." He prayed he still had one. Not only couldn't he make any promises to Lori, but he also couldn't even tell her his feelings.

"It is if you're living with her with our child. Maybe the judge should know, too."

"Stop with the threats, Shelly." He walked toward the front door. He opened the door and glanced out at the man on the porch and motioned to him to come inside.

Shelly looked at Jace suspiciously. "What are you up to?"

"You're the one who plays games, Shelly. So if I can't talk any sense into you, maybe he can." He prayed that all his hard work would pay off and not backfire in his face.

"Don't push me, Jace. You'll only lose." She gasped as Edmund Layfield stepped through the front door.

The distinguished gentleman was in his early fifties. He was dressed in a business suit and had thick gray hair. Jace had spent only an hour with the man and realized that he truly loved Shelly. Edmund also liked Cassie, but didn't particularly want to raise another child full-time, since his kids were grown.

Shelly came out of her trance. "Edmund, what are you doing here?"

"I came to see you, love. And I'm not leaving here until I convince you that we're meant to be together." He reached out and pulled her into his arms. That was when Jace made his exit.

For the first time in days, he realized that maybe they could come to a compromise. They all might get what they wanted. His thoughts turned to Lori. And that included him.

Tim parked the small SUV next to several other cars at Hutchinson House. It was Thanksgiving and half the town had been invited to have dinner here.

"Are you okay with this?" he asked Claire.

She smiled. "Normally no, but I can share this special day with Lori and Gina. It's important they feel a part of Destiny." She sighed. "Besides, all the kids and grandkids will be here." She smiled. "It's all about family being together. If only we would hear from Jace. You'd think our own daughter could give us some information."

He reached across the car and took his wife's hand. "Come on, Claire, you know Paige is Jace's lawyer."

"I know, I know, client/lawyer confidentiality." She frowned. "But I've seen how sad Lori is. If two people should be together, it's them."

"And if it's meant to be it will work out."

"I've been praying so hard for that."

It had been a week, and not a word from Jace. Lori had tried to stay positive—after all, it was Thanksgiving.

She looked around the festive dining room. The long table could seat twenty. There were two other tables set up in the entry to seat another twenty. And with the kids' table in the sunroom off the kitchen, everyone would have a place.

Maggie had cooked three turkeys and with Claire's two baked hams and many side dishes from everyone, she couldn't imagine not having enough food.

"Miss Hutchinson."

Lori turned to see Mac Burleson. "Mac, I asked you to call me Lori."

"Doesn't seem right," he told her.

"It seems very right to me. Unless you don't consider me a friend."

His eyes rounded. "You're a very good friend. I'm so grateful—"

"You did it," she interrupted. "You proved yourself at every job you've taken on. You make us all proud."

"Thank you…Lori." He smiled. "Is there anything else you want me to do?"

Some laughing kids ran by, chasing each other. She smiled at their antics. Her father would probably hate this. "Enjoy today. We have a lot to be thankful for." She knew she was so lucky, but two important people weren't here to share it with her.

"Hurry, Daddy, we're gonna be late for Thanksgiving."

Jace smiled, but it didn't relax him as he drove his

truck down First Street toward Hutchinson House. "We'll get there, sweetheart."

He glanced toward the backseat where his daughter was strapped in. They'd been gone a week, having stayed in Denver longer than planned. With the lawyers' help, they'd worked out the custody issue without a judge having to make the decision.

And in the end, it had been Cassie who'd told her mother that she wanted to live in Destiny with her daddy and all her friends and her horse. Shelly finally agreed, but wanted visitation in the summers and holidays. So Jace became the custodial parent. There was only one other thing that could make him happier. Lori.

"I just can't wait to see Ellie and Mrs. K. and Miss Lori, to tell everybody that I get to live here and be in the Christmas pageant."

"I can't wait, either," he told his daughter, praying that a certain pretty blonde felt the same about the news.

"Daddy, are you gonna ask Miss Lori today?"

On the flight home, Jace had told her how he felt about Lori and about her being a part of their lives. That was crazy, considering he hadn't even talked with Lori yet.

"Not sure. There's going to be a lot of people there today. It might have to wait, so you have to keep it a secret, okay?"

"Okay, but could I tell Ellie about Mommy's wedding? And that I'm going to go visit a real castle this summer?"

He smiled. "Yes, about the wedding, but the castle is only going to happen if I can get time off work." He was definitely going with her. He hoped Lori could go, too.

His heart began to race as he pulled up and climbed

out of the truck. He grabbed the wine and hurried after his daughter to the front door.

When they rang the bell, the door opened and Zack poked his head out. "Hi, Cassie. Hi, Mr. Jace."

"Hi, Zack. We came for Thanksgiving."

The boy grinned and opened the door wider and allowed them into the entryway filled with a long table decorated with colorful flowers and a paper turkey centerpiece. Cassie took off before he could stop her.

Jace was soon greeted by Justin and Morgan, then Tim Keenan and Paige and Reed Larkin joined them. He wanted to join in the conversation, but his eyes kept searching for a glimpse of Lori.

"She's in the kitchen."

He glanced at Justin. "Who?"

"As if you two are fooling anyone," his friend said. "You need to go to Lori before she comes out here and sees you."

Jace nodded and took off toward the kitchen. He knew his way around this house, but there were so many people here it was hard to maneuver. How was he going to be able to get her alone?

He saw Maggie at the counter. Without asking anything, she nodded toward the sunroom. He walked there as kids ran past him. Okay, so they weren't going to have any privacy.

Then he saw her and everyone else seemed to disappear from view. She was seated on the floor with some of the little kids. She was holding a toddler who'd been crying, and she managed to turn the tears into a smile before the child wandered off. Jace fell in love with her all over again.

Lori stood. Dressed in black slacks and a soft blue

sweater he ached to pull her close and just hold her. Tell her how much he'd missed her. How much he wanted her…

She finally turned in his direction. Her hair was in an array of curls that danced around her pretty face. Her chocolate eyes locked on his. "You're back."

That was a dumb thing to say, Lori thought as she looked up at Jace. So much for cool and calm.

"Hello, Lori."

"Hi, Jace." She didn't take a step toward him. "Is Cassie with you? Please tell me that she's with you."

He beamed. "Yes, she is." He glanced around. "I need to talk to you. There are so many things I have to tell you."

Just then Maggie broke in. "Sorry to interrupt but dinner is on the table. And Tim Keenan is ready to say the blessing."

Lori glanced back at Jace. "I'm sorry. Can we talk later?" Without waiting for an answer, Lori took off and headed toward the front of the house. She felt Jace following behind her as they reached the dining room. Hopeful, she added an extra place at the table for him.

She smiled at all her family and the new friends she was sharing today with. That included Jace and Cassie.

It grew quiet and someone handed her a champagne glass. "First of all, Gina, Zack and I want to thank you all for coming today. I hope this is the first of many visits to Hutchinson House. I want you all to feel welcome, so you'll come back here." She raised her glass. "To friends, and to Destiny." After everyone took a drink, she had Tim Keenan say the blessing.

The group broke up, and mothers went off to fill

their children's plates and settle them in the sunroom. Maggie stood by, watching for any emergencies. Lori ended up back at the head table, while Gina was seated at the entry table. Somehow Jace was seated at her table, but at the opposite end. Every so often, he'd smile at her.

She kept telling herself in a few hours they could be alone. After dinner, she went into the kitchen to check on dessert and finally saw Cassie.

"Miss Lori." The girl came and hugged her. "I got to come back."

"I know. Your daddy told me."

"Did he tell you about the wedding?" Cassie's tiny hand slapped over her mouth. "Oh, no, I wasn't supposed to tell you about that."

"Whose wedding? Your mommy's?" When Cassie didn't answer, she asked, "Your daddy's?"

The child giggled. "Both of 'em. But don't tell Daddy I told you. It's a surprise."

Lori could barely take her next breath. Was that why Jace said he got Cassie? He had to remarry Shelly?

She couldn't do this. She turned and found Jace behind her, holding her coat. "Okay, we need to get out of here and talk." He grinned. "I know just the place."

She gasped. "There's no need to tell me. I already heard from Cassie about the wedding. I hope you and Shelly will be happy."

He frowned. "What? You think that Shelly and I…" He cursed.

Lori held up her hand to stop him, but he took it in his.

"We're definitely going to talk about this," he began. "We need to get a few things straightened out. Now."

"I can't leave now."

"So we should just talk here. I'm sure all your guests would love to hear what I have to say," he said, and held out her coat.

"Why are you doing this?" she asked, keeping her voice low.

"I hate the fact that you even have to ask. I hope I can change that." When she hesitated, he asked, "Can't you even give me a few minutes to hear me out? To listen to what I have to say."

Lori wasn't sure what to do, only that she didn't want a scene here. She slipped on her coat and told Maggie she was leaving for a little while.

The housekeeper smiled and waved them on saying, "It's about time."

CHAPTER THIRTEEN

Twenty minutes later, Jace was still furious as he pulled off the highway. The sun had already set, but he knew the way to the cabin.

"Why are you bringing me here?" Lori asked.

"So we can talk without anyone interrupting us." He glanced across the bench seat. "But if you want, I'll take you back home."

He watched her profile in the shadowed light. She closed her eyes then whispered, "No, it might be good if we talk. At least to clear the air."

"Oh, darlin', I plan to do more than clear the air."

Lori jerked her head around and even in the darkness he could see she was glaring. She opened her mouth but he stopped her words.

"Hold that thought. We're here." He pulled into the parking space and climbed out. No more snow had fallen since the last time he'd followed her here. It hadn't gotten any warmer, either.

He pulled his sheepskin coat together to ward off the cold as he went around to Lori's side. After helping her out, they hurried up to the lit porch. He took the key from his pocket and rushed on to explain, "I stopped by earlier." He unlocked the door, pushed it open and turned on the light inside the door.

"After you," he told her, watching surprise cross her pretty face. "Come on, let's get inside where it's warm."

Lori felt Jace's hand against her back, nudging her in. Once inside she stopped and looked around, trying not to think about the last time they'd been here. It didn't work. Memories flooded her head. How incredible it had been being in Jace's arms, making love with him.

"Just let me get a fire started." Jace went straight to the fireplace, where logs had been placed on the grate. He turned on the gas and the flames shot over the wood. He lit the candles that were lined up along the mantel, then turned to her. "You should be warm in a few minutes."

She recalled another time he hadn't waited for the fire to warm her. She pushed away the thought and walked to the table where she saw a vase of fresh flowers. Red roses. She faced him. "You bought these?"

He nodded.

"So you'd planned to bring me here?"

He pulled off his jacket and went to her. "I've been thinking about it since I left Denver. I want to be with you alone, to talk to you."

With her heart racing, she returned to the fire and held out her hands to warm them. Mostly, she wanted to gather her thoughts, but she was overwhelmed by this man. She wanted to be hopeful, but she also recalled what Jace had told her. He didn't want to get involved with another woman.

"Are you ready to listen to what I have to say?"

She stared into the fire. "So now you want to talk?

Why didn't you call me before? Let me know what was going on."

"Because I didn't know myself until recently. I was in mediation during the day with Shelly and her lawyers. At night, I was trying to ease my daughter's fears." His sapphire gaze met hers. "And I guess I've been so used to doing things on my own, I didn't know how to depend on someone else."

"You didn't have to be alone. I was here for you."

"I know that now. Yet, in the end, I had to make the decision based on my daughter's well-being. It was hard to know what was best for Cassie. Was I being selfish wanting her with me?"

Hearing his stress, she turned, but didn't go to him. "Oh, Jace. No, you weren't being selfish. You love Cassie enough to want to give her stability. I also believe that you love your daughter enough that if Shelly could give Cassie what she needed, you'd let her have custody."

He smiled. "It always amazes me how you seem to know me so well."

That wasn't true, she thought, praying he wanted the same thing she did. To be together. "Not so. I have no idea why you brought me here, especially since I haven't heard a word in the past week. And what about this wedding?"

This time he came to her. He stood so close, she could inhale his wonderful scent. The only sounds were the logs crackling in the fire as she waited for an explanation.

Then he took her hand. "I might have helped a little with a nudge to Edmund. He took it from there and went to see Shelly. They were married yesterday by the same judge who helped with the custody case. I escorted Cassie to her mother's wedding."

"Shelly got married?"

"Yes. I thought things would go smoother if I helped Shelly settle her problem with her now-husband. I contacted him the day I arrived, and got him to come with me to Shelly's place." He shrugged. "They took it from there, and now they're headed to England for their honeymoon and his family."

Jace met her dark eyes and nearly lost his concentration. "Before Shelly left we managed to sit down and decide what would be best for our daughter. In the end, Cassie told her mother she wanted to live with me in Destiny."

"That had to be hard on Shelly."

Jace nodded. "But she gets visitation, summers and holidays. She can't take Cassie out of the country until she's older." He studied Lori's pretty face and his stomach tightened. He wanted her desperately.

"It all finally got settled yesterday, and Cassie and I caught the first flight back here…and came to see you."

He reached for her hand and tugged her closer. "I want more, Lori. More than just having my daughter in my life. I also want you. No, not just want you, but need you."

Not giving her a chance to resist, his mouth came down on hers in an all-consuming kiss. He couldn't resist her, either. His hands moved over her back, going downward to her hips, drawing her against him.

With a gasp, she pulled back. "You're not playing fair," she accused.

"I want you, Lorelei Hutchinson. I'll use any means possible to have you."

"Wait." Lori pushed him away, not liking this. "What are you exactly talking about? Seduction?" She deserved more. "I won't be that secret woman in your life, Jace, that you pull out whenever it's convenient."

He frowned. "Whoa. Who said anything about that…" He stopped as if to regroup.

"First of all, I'm sorry that I ever made you feel that way. I asked a lot of you when I left here, and I know I should have called you. Believe me I wanted to, but I was so afraid that if I did, I'd confess how I felt about you. I didn't have a right yet. I needed all my concentration on Cassie. You and I both know what it's like to lose parents. I would do anything not to have that happen to my daughter." His gaze bore into hers. "No matter how much I care about you, Lori, I couldn't abandon my child and come to you." He swallowed. "No matter how much I wanted to. Not matter how much I love you."

She closed her eyes.

"No, look at me, Lori. I'm not your father. I'm never going to leave you, ever. How could I when I can't seem to be able to live without you. Even if I had to move back to Denver because of Cassie, I would have figured out a way to come and be with you, too."

"You love me?"

He drew her close and nodded. "From the top of your pretty blond hair, to your incredible brown eyes, down to your cute little ruby-red painted toes." He kissed her forehead, then brushed his lips against each eyelid. His mouth continued a journey to her cheek, then she shivered as he reached her ear. "I'll tell you about all your other delicious body parts later," he promised, then pulled back and looked down at her. "If you'll let me."

"Oh, Jace. I love you, too," she whispered.

"I was hoping you felt that way." He pulled her into his arms and kissed her deeply. By the time he released her they were both breathing hard.

"We better slow down a minute, or I'll forget what I was about to do." He went to his coat and pulled a small box out of his jacket pocket, then returned to Lori.

Her eyes grew round. "Jace?"

He felt a little shaky. "I want this to be perfect, but if I manage to mess up something, just remember how much I love you." He drew a breath. "Lorelei Hutchinson, I probably can't offer you a perfect life. I have a home that's still under construction. A business that isn't off the ground yet." His eyes met hers. "And a daughter that I'm going to ask you to be a mother to."

A tear ran down her cheek. "Oh, Jace, don't you know, those are assets. And I couldn't love Cassie any more than if she were my own."

"She loves you, too."

"So she's okay with me and you?"

He nodded. "She even approved of the ring." He opened the box and she gasped at the square-cut diamond solitaire with the platinum band.

"Oh, my. It's beautiful."

That was his cue. He got down on one knee. "Lorelei Hutchinson, you are my heart. Will you marry me?"

She touched his face with her hands and kissed him softly. "Yes, Jace, oh, yes."

With her mouth still against his, he rose and wrapped his arms around her as he deepened the kiss. He couldn't let her go. Ever.

He finally broke off the kiss, then slipped the ring on her finger. He kissed her softly, then pulled back. "Give me one second, then we'll have the rest of the night."

Lori nodded and looked down at her ring. She couldn't believe this was really happening. "Good, I'm going to need your full attention the rest of the night to convince me that this isn't a fairy tale."

He grinned, took out his cell phone and punched in a number. "You got it." He put it to his ear. "Hi, sweetheart," Jace said into the receiver. "She said yes." He looked at Lori and winked. "Yes, we'll celebrate tomorrow. I love you, too." He ended the call. "I hope you don't mind. Cassie wanted to know what your answer was."

"I don't mind at all. I think we have enough love that I can share it with your daughter." She wrapped her arms around his waist. "But maybe tonight, I'll let you show me."

"Not just tonight, Lori. Always. Forever."

EPILOGUE

I⊤ WAS nearly Christmas in Destiny.

This year, the town council had asked Lori to light the big tree in the town square. She was honored, to say the least. Of course, she didn't do it alone. She'd invited Zack and Cassie to help throw the switch that lit the fifty-foot ponderosa pine.

While enjoying the colorful light show and the children's choir singing carols, she recalled the first day she'd arrived in Destiny. She felt so alone, then she started meeting the people here. That included one stubborn contractor who made her heart race. Made her aware of what she'd been missing in life.

For Lori there were bittersweet memories, too. Her father was gone and she'd never had the chance to have a relationship with him. But with her new family, she wasn't going to be alone. Not only Gina and Zack, but also her future husband, Jace, and a stepdaughter, Cassie.

Suddenly she felt a pair of arms slip around her waist from behind. She smiled and leaned back against Jace's broad chest.

"So are you enjoying your big night?" he said against her ear.

"Oh, yes." She smiled, recalling the last time she'd been here with her father. She called them treasured memories now. "But I have to say, I'm glad the school play is over."

"Until next year," he reminded her.

"Very funny. I'm planning to be really busy."

"You do too much as it is," he said as they watched the children's choir singing beside the tree. He tightened his hold, his large body shielding her from the cold night. "Between the mortgage and college scholarship programs, you have no free time."

She and Jace had made the decision together about taking only a small part of the inheritance to put away for the kids; the rest would go back into the town. They both made an excellent income from Hutchinson Corp properties.

"I want to get the programs up and ready for when my father's money comes through next fall." She stole a glance over her shoulder at him. "You'd be proud of me. I've turned over my job on the mortgage committee to Erin. She'll go to all the meetings, and I'll work from her recommendations."

"However you get it done, you're a pretty special lady to be so generous to this town."

She turned in his arms. "I only want to be your special lady."

He grew serious. "You are, Lori, and will always be." He kissed her sweetly. "How about we ditch this place for something a little more private."

"Oh, I'd like that, but you know we can't. For one thing, Cassie and Zack are singing." They both looked at the children. "And we're all invited back to the Keenan Inn for a party and to finalize our wedding plans. It's going to be a big undertaking for Claire and Gina to pull this off, especially with the holidays."

"I know, the first wedding at Hutchinson House," he said.

"The first of many, I hope," she reminded him.

Jace had to smile. With the exception of Cassie's birth, he couldn't remember ever being this happy. Now he had it all, the woman he loved and his daughter permanently. "So I guess a wild night together is out of the question."

"Of course not. It's just postponed for a few weeks."

"Until New Year's Eve," he finished. The date they'd chosen for their wedding. "That's a long three weeks off." Even longer since they'd spent most of their time with Cassie trying to help her adjust to the new arrangement. He hated having to send Lori home every night.

"You sure we can't sneak off to the cabin tonight?"

She gave him a quick kiss. "Just hold that thought and I promise to make it worth your while after the wedding."

"You being here with me now has made my dreams come true."

Hutchinson House never looked so beautiful.

On New Year's Eve Lori stood at the window of the master suite. She could see over the wide yard toward the front of the property.

The ornate gates were covered with thousands of tiny silver lights and many more were strung along the hedges. It was only a prelude for what was to come as the wedding guests approached the end of the circular drive and the grand house on the hill.

The porch railings were draped in fresh garland, and

more lights were intermixed with the yards of green-ery that smelled of Christmas. White poinsettias edged the steps leading to the wide front door trimmed with a huge fresh-cut wreath.

Lori smiled. The Hutchinson/Yeager wedding was going to be the first of many parties in this house.

Gina came in dressed in a long dark green grown. "Oh, Lori. You look so beautiful."

Lori glanced down at her wedding dress. She'd fallen in love with the floor-length ivory gown the second she'd seen it at Rocky Mountain Bridal Shop, from the top of the sweetheart neckline, to the fitted jeweled bodice with a drop waist and satin skirt. Her hair was pulled back, adorned with a floral headband attached to a long tulle veil.

"I hope Jace thinks so."

Gina handed her a deep red rose bouquet. "He will."

She felt tears forming. "I'm so lucky to have found him, and Cassie."

Gina blinked, too. "They're lucky to have you." She gripped Lori's hand. "I love you, sis. Thank you for al-ways being there for us."

"Hey, you were there for me, too. And nothing will change. We're still family. I'm only going to be a few miles from your new place." Lori frowned, knowing they had arranged to live in their own house. "You feel okay about the move?"

Her sister nodded. "Zack and I are going to be fine."

Lori knew that. Her sister was working with Kaley, having hours that enabled her to be home when Zack got out of school. She still worried about Eric showing up someday, but they'd all keep an eye out.

Gina straightened. "Okay, let's get your special day started."

They walked into the hall toward the head of the stairs where Charlie was waiting. She couldn't lie, every girl dreamed of walking down the aisle escorted by her father. She wasn't any different. At least now she'd been able to make peace with it all.

She whispered, "I'll always miss you, Dad."

Smiling, Charlie had tears in his eyes when she arrived. "Oh, Miss Lorelei, you are a vision. I'm so honored to escort you today."

She gripped his hands. "Thank you, Charlie."

The older man offered her his arm. "I know there's an anxious young man waiting for his bride."

The music began and Cassie and Zack, the flower girl and ring bearer, started down the petal-covered stairs. The banister entwined with more garland that wound down to the large entry. Next Gina began her descent. Once her sister reached the bottom the music swelled.

Holding tight on to Charlie, Lori's heart raced when she made her way down. Once she touched the bottom steps, she took it all in.

The room was filled with flowers: roses, carnations and poinsettias, all white. Rows of wooden chairs, filled with family and friends, lined either side of the runner that led through the entry and into the dining room and ended at a white trellis covered in greenery. And underneath stood Jace. The man who was going to share her life.

Jace's breath caught when his gaze met Lori's. She was beautiful. His heart swelled. He never knew he could love someone so much.

She made her way to him and he had to stop himself from going to her. Finally she arrived and he took her hand. When he locked on her big brown eyes, everything else seemed to fade away. There was only her. It was just the two of them exchanging vows, making the life commitment.

The minister began the ceremony and the vows were exchanged. Jace listened to her speak and was humbled by her words.

Then came his turn. He somehow managed to get the emotional words past his tight throat. Then Justin passed him the ring, and he slipped the platinum band on her finger. He held out his hand so she could do the same.

He gripped both her hands and the minister finally pronounced them husband and wife. Jace leaned down, took her in his arms and kissed her.

There were cheers as the minister announced, "It's my pleasure to introduce to you, Mr. and Mrs. Jace Yeager."

Jace held his bride close, never wanting to let her go. She was his heart, his life, the mother of his future children.

It had been a long journey but they had found each other. He pulled back and looked at his bride. "Hello, Mrs. Yeager."

With tears in her eyes, she answered, "Hello, Mr. Yeager."

Together they walked down the aisle hand in hand past the well-wishers toward their future together. It was their Destiny.

* * * * *

Mills & Boon® Hardback

October 2012

ROMANCE

Banished to the Harem	Carol Marinelli
Not Just the Greek's Wife	Lucy Monroe
A Delicious Deception	Elizabeth Power
Painted the Other Woman	Julia James
A Game of Vows	Maisey Yates
A Devil in Disguise	Caitlin Crews
Revelations of the Night Before	Lynn Raye Harris
Defying her Desert Duty	Annie West
The Wedding Must Go On	Robyn Grady
The Devil and the Deep	Amy Andrews
Taming the Brooding Cattleman	Marion Lennox
The Rancher's Unexpected Family	Myrna Mackenzie
Single Dad's Holiday Wedding	Patricia Thayer
Nanny for the Millionaire's Twins	Susan Meier
Truth-Or-Date.com	Nina Harrington
Wedding Date with Mr Wrong	Nicola Marsh
The Family Who Made Him Whole	Jennifer Taylor
The Doctor Meets Her Match	Annie Claydon

MEDICAL

A Socialite's Christmas Wish	Lucy Clark
Redeeming Dr Riccardi	Leah Martyn
The Doctor's Lost-and-Found Heart	Dianne Drake
The Man Who Wouldn't Marry	Tina Beckett

0912 GEN STD HB

Mills & Boon® Large Print

October 2012

ROMANCE

A Secret Disgrace	Penny Jordan
The Dark Side of Desire	Julia James
The Forbidden Ferrara	Sarah Morgan
The Truth Behind his Touch	Cathy Williams
Plain Jane in the Spotlight	Lucy Gordon
Battle for the Soldier's Heart	Cara Colter
The Navy SEAL's Bride	Soraya Lane
My Greek Island Fling	Nina Harrington
Enemies at the Altar	Melanie Milburne
In the Italian's Sights	Helen Brooks
In Defiance of Duty	Caitlin Crews

HISTORICAL

The Duchess Hunt	Elizabeth Beacon
Marriage of Mercy	Carla Kelly
Unbuttoning Miss Hardwick	Deb Marlowe
Chained to the Barbarian	Carol Townend
My Fair Concubine	Jeannie Lin

MEDICAL

Georgie's Big Greek Wedding?	Emily Forbes
The Nurse's Not-So-Secret Scandal	Wendy S. Marcus
Dr Right All Along	Joanna Neil
Summer With A French Surgeon	Margaret Barker
Sydney Harbour Hospital: Tom's Redemption	Fiona Lowe
Doctor on Her Doorstep	Annie Claydon

ROMANCE

MEDICAL

Mills & Boon® Large Print

November 2012

ROMANCE

The Secrets She Carried	Lynne Graham
To Love, Honour and Betray	Jennie Lucas
Heart of a Desert Warrior	Lucy Monroe
Unnoticed and Untouched	Lynn Raye Harris
Argentinian in the Outback	Margaret Way
The Sheikh's Jewel	Melissa James
The Rebel Rancher	Donna Alward
Always the Best Man	Fiona Harper
A Royal World Apart	Maisey Yates
Distracted by her Virtue	Maggie Cox
The Count's Prize	Christina Hollis

HISTORICAL

An Escapade and an Engagement	Annie Burrows
The Laird's Forbidden Lady	Ann Lethbridge
His Makeshift Wife	Anne Ashley
The Captain and the Wallflower	Lyn Stone
Tempted by the Highland Warrior	Michelle Willingham

MEDICAL

Sydney Harbour Hospital: Lexi's Secret	Melanie Milburne
West Wing to Maternity Wing!	Scarlet Wilson
Diamond Ring for the Ice Queen	Lucy Clark
No.1 Dad in Texas	Dianne Drake
The Dangers of Dating Your Boss	Sue MacKay
The Doctor, His Daughter and Me	Leonie Knight